SHARPSHOOTER McCLURE

US Marshal Jesse Cole sends deputy sheriff Mike McClure to infiltrate the hired guns harassing the homesteaders of Harmony. But a night of bloody carnage ends in failure with the marshal dead. Mike escapes but, trailed by the gunslingers, Mike assumes a new identity, working with Brandon Webb's Wild West Show. However, memories of that terrible night ensure his return to Harmony. He'll need all his gun skills to bring the guilty parties to justice.

Books by I. J. Parnham
in the Linford Western Library:

THE OUTLAWED DEPUTY
THE LAST RIDER FROM HELL
BAD DAY IN DIRTWOOD
DEVINE'S LAW
YATES'S DILEMMA
DEAD BY SUNDOWN
CALHOUN'S BOUNTY
CALLOWAY'S CROSSING
BAD MOON OVER DEVIL'S RIDGE
MASSACRE AT BLUFF POINT
THE GALLOWS GANG
RIDERS OF THE BARREN PLAINS

I. J. PARNHAM

SHARPSHOOTER McCLURE

Complete and Unabridged

LINFORD
Leicester

First published in Great Britain in 2010 by
Robert Hale Limited
London

First Linford Edition
published 2011
by arrangement with
Robert Hale Limited
London

British Library CIP Data

Parnham, I. J.
    Sharpshooter McClure. - -
    (Linford western library)
    1. Western stories.
    2. Large type books.
    I. Title II. Series
    823.9′2–dc22

    ISBN 978–1–44480–513–0

Published by
F. A. Thorpe (Publishing)
Anstey, Leicestershire

Set by Words & Graphics Ltd.
Anstey, Leicestershire
Printed and bound in Great Britain by
T. J. International Ltd., Padstow, Cornwall

This book is printed on acid-free paper

Prologue

Jesse Cole hunched forward in the saddle, his right eye twitching with an insistent rhythm as he entered his second hour of waiting. Beyond the entrance to the gully, twilight redness painted a long swath across the western horizon. With every drop in the light-level his irritation increased.

He had just decided he would have to leave his hiding place and risk heading into Prudence after all, when Clyde Kilgore came riding through the gully entrance.

'At last,' he muttered to himself and urged his horse on to meet him.

As he'd expected Clyde was singing enthusiastically while swaying from side to side in the saddle, showing he'd used his extra time in town to maximum effect.

'Howdy there, partner,' Clyde called out, liquor slurring his speech.

'You're late,' Jesse said, drawing his horse to a halt.

Clyde rode by him. While waving his hat in the air he leant from the saddle to keep Jesse in his view. The change in his posture almost made him fall to the ground. With a pronounced lurch he righted himself, then swung his horse around to come to an uncertain halt beside him.

'I surely am,' he declared. His whiskey-laden breath washed over Jesse even from several yards away.

With one bleary eye open and the other closed he considered Jesse, then fumbled in his pocket and produced a half-empty bottle of whiskey. He held it out, but received only a piercing glare. That didn't deter Clyde and, while grinning, he uncorked then upended the bottle.

Jesse was minded to knock the bottle from his grasp, but they had a long journey ahead of them and he didn't want to waste any more time by starting an argument.

'If you've finished enjoying yourself,' he said, 'we have to go.'

'Lighten up and enjoy life.' Clyde held the bottle up to the light to see how much was left, then pocketed it and wiped his mouth with the back of his hand. 'We could end up dead before the week is out, and dead men don't get to enjoy whiskey.'

'In my experience men who enjoy whiskey end up dead.'

Jesse moved on, but then drew back on the reins, his warning perhaps proving to be a valid one sooner than he had expected.

A rider was facing them in the entrance to the gully, his form silhouetted against the twilit sky beyond.

The sight silenced Clyde. With a roll of his shoulders he tried to shake off his drunken state.

'What you want?' he shouted, facing the newcomer. 'Why are you . . . ?'

Jesse grunted at Clyde to be quiet, then watched the rider move his horse on to approach them. With the lighter sky behind him Jesse couldn't discern his features until he stopped ten yards from them. He appeared to be young, his face so fresh-faced that Jesse doubted he shaved.

'Like he said, what do you want, kid?' he asked.

'I'm not a kid,' the newcomer said, his voice deep enough to suggest he was telling the truth. 'I'm Mike McClure, the deputy sheriff of Prudence, and this man is under arrest for petty larceny and assault.'

Jesse couldn't help but snort. 'You're no lawman, kid.'

'I have no quarrel with you, but if you don't move aside, I'll arrest you too.'

Jesse glanced at Clyde, to see that he was muttering to himself while glaring at the newcomer. Clearly his excessive drinking wasn't helping him to think rationally, so Jesse wasn't surprised when he threw his hand to his gun.

Before Jesse had decided how he should react, the deputy drew, then blasted a slug that winged Clyde's hand as he slipped his gun from its holster. The gun went flying.

Clyde cried out in pain and jerked his bloodstained hand to his face to inspect the damage, but long before the gun had hit the ground the lawman had turned his gun on Jesse.

'Nice shooting, kid,' Jesse said, 'but you just made the biggest mistake of your young life.'

'If you don't raise those hands, you'll have made the biggest mistake of your old life.'

As Jesse sized up his opponent, judging whether he was speaking out of bravado, Clyde licked his wound, wincing, then darted a glance at him.

'You're not going to let him arrest me, are you, Jesse?'

Jesse shrugged. 'I reckon this trigger-happy kid and his drawn gun gives me no choice.'

'As I told you, I'm not a kid,' the deputy muttered. 'I'm a lawman.'

Jesse considered his wounded and

aggrieved colleague, then the young lawman. With a long sigh he moved his horse on to approach him.

'You may be a lawman, kid,' he said, lowering his voice, 'but the trouble is, so am I, and you've just ruined two weeks of hard work.'

1

Mike McClure threw his prisoner into a cell then locked the door and turned away to find out whether Marshal Jesse Cole was still irate. He got his answer soon enough when the marshal slapped his hands down on Sheriff Simmons's desk and darted his head forward like an angry rattler.

'How long have you let that kid do this job?' he demanded, while pointing at Mike.

Mike started to speak, aiming to clarify his actions, but Simmons raised a hand to silence him.

'Mike's no kid, he's just a fresh-faced twenty-year-old,' Simmons said. He considered the US marshal, then leaned back in his chair. 'But if you're that interested in his record, I deputized him last week. In that time he's completed every task I've given him and shown himself to be a fast learner.'

Mike relaxed, pleased to hear that even after his unfortunate mistake he had Simmons's support, but it did nothing to appease the marshal, who stood back from the desk, sneering.

'So I have to have my operation ruined and people have to die so he can learn how to slam drunken yahoos like Clyde in jail, is that it?'

Simmons shrugged and when he spoke he still used his usual level tone.

'If I had a dime for every time a lawman rode into my town and blamed me for his failings, I could retire. You should have told me what you were doing, then I wouldn't have sent him off to arrest Clyde.'

Jesse gritted his teeth. With a long sigh he looked aloft then nodded slowly.

'I guess you might have yourself a point,' he said, lowering his voice, 'but that doesn't change the fact that Clyde now knows I'm a lawman.'

'What were you investigating?' Simmons asked, matching Jesse's more conciliatory tone.

Jesse sat on the edge of the sheriff's desk and glanced at the prisoner in the cell, who was now sitting up on his cot and glaring at them all.

'A rancher called Nyle Adams over in Harmony.'

'Everybody knows of Nyle. He's the biggest rancher north of Prudence. What's he done?'

'Nyle's not content with being the biggest. He wants more land. Six months ago he hired the gunslinger Floyd Kelly to drive away the homesteaders who bordered his territory. Floyd intimidated them so well nobody would talk even after a family burnt to death in their own home. Now, with Nyle hiring more guns, his campaign is set to get even bloodier. So I aimed to put a stop to his activities by infiltrating Floyd's gang.'

Simmons nodded towards the cells. 'And Clyde is one of those guns?'

'Yup. I earned his trust and he was prepared to talk me into the gang, but he won't after that trigger-happy kid arrested him.'

Simmons beckoned for Mike to join them, then got up from his chair to stand beside him, providing an obvious and welcome gesture of support.

'My deputy here has the eyes of an eagle, but he's not trigger-happy.'

Simmons glanced at Mike, inviting him to speak.

'I'm not,' Mike said, choosing his words carefully to avoid inflaming the situation, 'and with a fine lawman like Sheriff Simmons helping me, I hope that one day I'll make a fine lawman too.'

Jesse frowned while looking him in the eye for the first time since he'd arrested Clyde.

'I guess gun-toting kids like you don't often choose the way of the law.'

'They sure don't,' Mike said, smiling and hoping a light joke would reduce the tension, 'so you should be grateful that if nothing else, you won't ever have to face me in no showdown.'

The comment made Jesse scowl, but Simmons swung round to look at him, his brow furrowing. Then he went to the window and stood looking out, his hands behind his back in a gesture that meant he was mulling over something.

After a few moments Simmons turned and thumped a fist into his palm with a resounding slap.

'You're right, Marshal,' he said. 'Young men like Mike often become gunslingers. So why not let him become one?'

'What do you mean?' Jesse asked, cautiously.

Simmons went on to outline his idea to the increasingly exasperated marshal. Mike was disappointed to see that it rekindled the argument that appeared to have been resolved.

With him being forgotten about as the two senior lawmen bickered, Mike busied himself with some paperwork until the softly spoken sheriff talked the marshal round to his way of thinking. And the marshal's acquiescence brought with it news that was even more surprising.

'*You* want to deputize *me*?' Mike murmured, aghast, his heart beating faster.

'Against my better judgement, I do,' Jesse said. 'But that's only because I can't think of a better idea. Nyle Adams is expecting two gunslingers and even if Clyde isn't one of them, there's a small chance he'll accept you instead. And a small chance is better than none.'

'Well I'll be a . . . ' Mike gave up trying to appear calm and punched the air with glee. 'Last week I got made a deputy sheriff and now I'm a deputy US Marshal!'

'It's a temporary assignment, kid. I'm making you a special deputy for this job only.'

'I'm not a . . . ' Mike bit his lip. 'I'll be ready to leave within the hour.'

'You'll be ready to leave within five minutes.'

With that order Jesse headed outside. Mike shot a glance at Sheriff Simmons, who gave him an encouraging smile.

'This is your chance to make amends,' he said. 'Take it.'

Mike nodded and as ordered five minutes later he was mounted up and ready to leave town. Full darkness had descended, but that didn't deter his new boss and at a steady pace they rode out of town.

They'd ridden for several hours. From the position of the stars Mike judged it was around midnight when the marshal deemed that they'd made up for the time he'd lost and let them settle down.

Mike had accepted that the marshal didn't think too highly of him, so he stayed quiet, but when they'd settled down under their blankets Jesse spoke to him for the first time since they'd left town.

'So what made you think you could be a lawman?' he asked.

Mike noted that for the first time he hadn't referred to him as a kid. So, feeling heartened, he gave him a brief summary of his situation.

He had been twelve when while hunting he had found he had a steady and accurate aim. With both his parents dead, Uncle Bob, the man who looked after him, had encouraged him to hone those skills.

For the next eight years he'd employed his ability only to hunt, and even when he'd set out to find work he'd never considered doing anything with his talent until a chance encounter last week had changed his life.

On the way to Prudence he'd happened across a raider accosting two travellers. The raider had already subdued them and was tying them up, but Mike's intervention had ensured he didn't benefit from his crime.

He'd prepared himself, sneaked up on the raider and shot the gun from his hand. That had been the first time he'd shot at a man. He had found it harder to do than shooting at prey, but the potential victims were delighted. Then, with their help, he'd taken the man into Prudence.

Sheriff Simmons had been so impressed with the tale the grateful travellers had related that he'd offered Mike the job of being his deputy sheriff.

'Having a keen eye gets you nowhere,' Jesse said when Mike had finished his tale, 'other than being dead real quick.'

'I'll back my sure aim to take on anything we have to face.'

Jesse considered him, shaking his head. 'I should never have let Simmons talk me into this.'

'Why?'

'Because I don't back your gun skills to help us none,' Jesse snapped. 'Experience is the only thing that'll keep us alive, and you've got none of that.'

Mike lowered his head, accepting that Jesse was right.

'If you don't accept my help,' he said, 'how will I ever get that experience?'

'You'll get it in the same way as I did

— by being lucky and by living for long enough to realize how lucky you've been.'

Mike could see that a badly thought-out retort could result in him having a long journey back to Prudence sooner than he wanted, so he acknowledged Jesse's concerns with a conciliatory smile and tone.

'All I can say is, I may not have much experience of the type of situation we're heading into, but I'll do everything you tell me to do, and I'm grateful you accepted my help.'

Jesse snorted. 'In a few days you might think otherwise.'

★   ★   ★

Ten miles out of the small town of Harmony, Mike and Jesse found the trading post in which they'd meet Nyle Adams and Floyd Kelly.

The ramshackle building was so dilapidated it looked as if it was awaiting a kindly wind to take pity on it and blow it away. But several horses were outside, making Jesse confident that the rancher and Kelly would be here.

'Keep quiet,' Jesse said as he dismounted, 'follow my lead, and you might live for long enough to be a deputy sheriff again.'

Mike nodded and followed Jesse inside. Wares were piled at one side of the post; a counter was at the other side.

Six men were leaning on the counter, sharing a whiskey bottle. Five of them turned to appraise the newcomers. They were all mean-eyed and rough-clad, adding further weight to Jesse's belief that they were the gunslingers Nyle Adams was recruiting.

Jesse walked past them to stand behind the one man who hadn't turned, he being the only smartly dressed man.

'Nyle Adams?' he said.

'Who wants to know?' the man said, still keeping his gaze set forward.

'The name's Jesse McGiven and this is Mike Shaw,' Jesse said, giving their agreed false names.

'I've heard of you.' Nyle turned and nodded to Jesse. Then he cast a long and sceptical look at Mike. 'But not him.'

Mike stood tall and returned Nyle's frank gaze.

'And I'd never heard of you,' he said, 'but Clyde Kilgore said you were hiring so I thought it worth my time to come.'

Nyle narrowed his eyes. 'Where is Clyde?'

Jesse shot Mike a harsh glare that warned him not to speak again, then spat on the floor.

'Damn varmint couldn't resist getting himself a whole heap of drinks then bruising a few jaws back in Prudence. That got him arrested by some snot-nosed kid with a deputy's star pinned to his scrawny chest.'

'That sounds like Clyde.' Nyle looked Jesse up and down, then did the same to Mike. 'And so that leaves me with the problem of what to do with you two.'

Jesse shrugged. 'Pay me well and I'll join you. Don't and I'll leave.'

'Clyde said you were the kind of man I'm looking for, so I'll pay.' He pointed at Mike. 'But not him.'

'Clyde picked him as his replacement. He said you wouldn't be disappointed.'

'I already am.' Nyle glanced at the nearest of his hired guns. 'But it's your decision, Floyd. You're the one who'll be using him.'

He turned his back on them, dismissing the matter. Accordingly, Floyd walked past Jesse to appraise Mike.

'You old enough to be let out on your own, son?' he asked.

Floyd's sneering gaze convinced Mike that he wouldn't get hired unless he proved his worth. So he looked at each of the hired guns, all of whom returned his gaze with studied contempt. Then he moved to lean on the counter, letting the motion mask him flicking his hand to his holster. A moment later his gun was in his hand and he'd thrust the barrel up under Floyd's chin. He pressed in so hard that Floyd had to raise himself up on to his tiptoes.

'You'll say that I am,' he muttered, 'or I'll be . . . annoyed.'

'Pulling a gun on me,' Floyd croaked, his chin held so high he found it hard to speak, 'was the worst mistake you've ever made.'

'For you it sure could be. I've ridden for three days on the promise of a good pay-off.' Mike edged the gun a mite higher and grinned. 'So if your boss doesn't live up to Clyde's promises, I'll splatter your brains all over the ceiling.'

'Take that gun off him,' Nyle said, turning to consider him, 'or my men will shoot you to hell.'

'Yeah,' Floyd said, then flicked his eyes to the side. 'And my newest recruit Jesse will be the first to tear a hole in you.'

Behind him the hired guns swung away from the counter to flank Floyd while Jesse paced round to confront him, his narrowed eyes and stern posture appearing to show that he was prepared to sacrifice him to prove his cover.

Mike gulped, but he kept his gun hand firm.

'That's a foolish threat to make,' he muttered, 'when my finger's on the trigger and what passes for your brains is on the wrong end of my gun. Now tell your boss to pay up or I'll show him how good I am by blasting these men to hell before you take another breath. And then I'll do the same to you and Nyle.'

Floyd locked gazes with him. Mike didn't know what he'd do if Floyd called his bluff, but thankfully Jesse snorted a laugh, then moved forward.

'Mike, stop playing the fool. It's not polite to threaten the man who'll pay you.' Still feigning a jovial tone and attitude he walked up to Floyd and spoke into his ear. 'You see the kid here may look a fresh-faced young green-horn, but you've seen that he's got a temper. Tell Nyle to hire him and you won't be disappointed.'

For long moments Floyd eyed Mike. Then he managed a slight nod. When this made the other men relax, Jesse flashed Mike a glance that warned him that this would be his only chance to back down.

So after glaring at Floyd for several heartbeats Mike lowered his gun, then holstered it. Floyd delivered an audible gulp as he rocked back down on to his heels.

'That was a wise move, son,' he said, rolling his shoulders.

'Don't make me regret it,' Mike said, figuring he should continue to behave in an arrogant manner.

Floyd nodded, seemingly dismissing the incident, and turned to Nyle. He beckoned for everyone to return to their business, making Mike sigh with relief now that his risky action had worked. But then, without warning, Floyd swirled round and hurled his fist backhanded at Mike's face.

The sudden action caught Mike unawares. Floyd's knuckles slapped him across the cheek.

The blow was glancing and not powerful enough to knock him over, but Floyd's follow-through punch that hit him squarely on the chin was. It crashed his jaw shut so firmly it felt as if his teeth had been knocked through the back of his head. He fell, poleaxed.

When Mike regained consciousness he was lying on his back and a pail of cold water was hitting him in the face with all the velocity of Floyd's fist. He shook himself and sat up. His blurred vision slowly focused on Floyd's face looming over him.

'And that's the trouble with all the hot-headed young gunslingers I've ever met,' Floyd said. 'The more arrogant they are, the quicker they die.'

'That mean,' Jesse said, 'you're not hiring the kid?'

Floyd laughed as he straightened up. 'I didn't say that. That temper of his will get him killed all too soon enough, but Nyle has given me a job to do and he's just the kind of headstrong fool I need to do it.'

Floyd snorted at the still groggy Mike, then turned to the counter and poured out a fresh round of drinks.

With the first part of his assignment complete, albeit not in the way he had thought it would be accomplished, Mike dragged himself to his feet. He leaned on the counter, catching his breath and not meeting anyone's eye.

Tentatively he rocked his jaw from side to side. His senses had fully returned when Nyle pushed a glass of whiskey down the bar to him.

'So,' Mike said raising the glass and continuing to act the role he'd carved out for himself, 'what is this job?'

'Recently the homesteaders on what should be my land have been getting too uppity,' Nyle said, addressing everyone. 'Their self-proclaimed leader is George Hughes. Tonight he's holding a meeting in Harmony where the dirt-grabbers will decide what trouble they'll cause me next. You're going to attend that meeting.'

'And do what?' Jesse asked, speaking up before Mike could think of the right thing to say.

Nyle smiled. 'The kid here will get a chance to do to George what he tried to do to Floyd.'

2

'What in tarnation are they doing?' Floyd Kelly murmured as he drew his horse to a halt on the outskirts of Harmony.

'I reckon they've laid on a show for us,' Jesse said.

Floyd sneered, then gestured for everyone to dismount and follow him into town.

Harmony was a small and decrepit settlement, containing a stable, a saloon and two other derelict buildings, but this evening it was packed with what Mike reckoned was all the nearby homesteaders.

Men, women and children sat huddled along the short main thoroughfare. They were hard-muscled and dirty from hard work, but tonight they were relaxing as they watched a group of people who were clearly from elsewhere. These people were gaudily-dressed and bright-eyed and when he got closer Mike saw the legend on one of their wagons, which proclaimed them as being members of Brandon Webb's Wild West Show.

Floyd and the others filed in at the back of the people watching outside the stable. Their presence attracted the kind of interest Mike expected, with the homesteaders and the showfolk looking at them with concern and some fear.

'What do you want, Floyd?' one homesteader said, standing up to shake a fist at them.

'Thought you'd be the first to complain, George Hughes,' Floyd said. 'But relax. We're here because we'd heard you were having a meeting tonight.'

'We are, but these kind people were passing through on the way to Redemption City and they offered to entertain us first.'

'Sounds mighty interesting,' Floyd said, his harsh tone suggesting the opposite. 'So sit down and let them entertain us too.'

George glared at the line of gunslingers, but with Floyd acting in such a non-confrontational manner, he sat back down, although he continued to glance their way.

After a few moments of uncomfortable silence one of the showfolk climbed on to a stage that had been erected before a blue-painted wagon.

'If everyone is ready,' he said, 'I am the legendary Brandon Webb and the show you are about to see is the greatest in all the world!'

With an overhead gesture he declared the show open and despite the seriousness of the mission Floyd had sent them on, Mike leaned back against the stable wall and did his best to enjoy what he saw.

The show started with a demonstration of riding skills. Two riders, Logan and Clifford, galloped down the road towards the recently set sun, then turned and stopped. With a flourish a woman removed the covers from two stakes that had been set in the road, to reveal hats.

The riders thundered back, leaned from the saddles, dragged the hats away, then twirled them on to their heads. Then they did a sharp turn, which made the horses rear before they galloped off back to their positions.

This manoeuvre received subdued applause, along with comments that that was something anyone could do.

Mike thought the same, but he hadn't considered Brandon's showmanship. The next time the riders came in they each had to snatch a flower from the woman's outstretched hands, which they did with ease before presenting them to women in the audience.

This made everyone sigh and relax. Thereafter the tasks became harder, subduing the deprecating comments until by the time they had to remove a kerchief from a knife set within a burning ring everyone except the gunslingers cheered.

When two new men, Dexter and

Sheridan, presented a demonstration of lassoing and ropetricks the townsfolk stopped casting looks at the gunslingers and began to enjoy the show with rapt attention.

The next performance was a sharpshooting display. This act didn't impress Mike. He reckoned he could shoot smaller targets from further away than Sharpshooter Clancy.

The spectators were impressed, but in keeping with the character he'd adopted he muttered deprecating comments to the gunslingers. Floyd grunted his approval of Mike's assessment.

Then, in keeping with the varied nature of the show, Brandon introduced the next act, which was performed by two Cheyennes, Big Man and Little Feather. She had a feather in her hair and moccasins on her feet along with a rawhide dress that was probably too short to be authentic. He sported a glorious mane of feathers.

After parading before the audience Big Man threw Little Feather over his shoulder and took her to a tall stake set in the ground. There a play-acted struggle that wasn't explained ensued, ending with him tying her to the stake. Then he threw knives at her.

By now Floyd was muttering to himself while casting aggrieved looks at George Hughes, making George shuffle uncomfortably.

Everyone else was impressed and every throw received a gasp from the audience as the knives sliced into the stake above her head or into the stakes on either side of her. The performance ended with Big Man's elaborate war dance while waving a tomahawk over his head, after which he threw that at her. The tomahawk whirled past her arm and stuck into another stake.

From Mike's position he could see that, as the tomahawk flew by, Little Feather twisted her wrists to remove her bonds, but it appeared to most of the audience that Big Man had cut the rope. When she fell into his arms, having proved her bravery by not

31

flinching, the townsfolk cheered, making the gunslingers grumble to each other, wondering when Floyd would act.

Full darkness had arrived when the woman who had removed the covers from the stakes earlier stepped up on to the stage. She sang a song. Unlike the previous acts, hers was a delicate and touching performance.

Mike wasn't surprised when Floyd chose this moment to register his displeasure at last.

'That's enough!' he shouted, his voice echoing in the road and cutting her off in mid-note. 'The show's over.'

'But I have more delights to present,' Brandon said, stepping up on to the stage to face Floyd. 'In fact I reckon you'll enjoy my dancing — '

'The show is over,' Floyd intoned. 'You can leave town or I can run you out of town. The choice is yours.'

Brandon backed away a pace while casting looks at his colleagues. They all returned significant glances that appeared silently to question whether they should escalate the confrontation. But before they could bring their deliberations to any conclusion George stood and took the attention away from them.

'These people kindly stopped in Harmony to entertain us,' he said. 'Not you.'

'This night is not about entertainment,' Floyd said. 'We came to give you a message from Nyle Adams. The longer this show goes on, the longer I have to wait to hear your reply.'

'Give us the message, we'll reply and then we'll go back to enjoying the show.'

'After this message, you won't be interested in no show.'

George and Floyd continued to shout taunts at each other across the road, but the argument had the required effect of dampening everyone's interest in the show. The showfolk caught on to the change in mood and began to pack up their wagons.

While they worked, the rest of the

menfolk gathered together. After conducting some terse conversations and exchanging concerned looks with the womenfolk, the women collected the children. At a slow pace they took them out of town and back to their homes, leaving the men to face Floyd.

Within half an hour Brandon's show had packed up and was heading away into the darkness. The only people left in town were Floyd and his six gunslingers, along with a dozen homesteaders.

George led the farmers into the stable where they picked up whatever tools and implements they found inside before gathering at the far end to look at the men in the doorway.

'No matter what the message is,' George said, 'this is our land and we'll fight to the last to keep it!'

His strident declaration encouraged the farmers to cheer and wave their pitchforks and spades above their heads.

Floyd Kelly took the lead while Mike

and Jesse stayed back to let the other men pace into the stable first. Then they filed in and stood against the back wall to await developments.

Floyd considered the farmers then looked over their heads to glare at George, his eyes cold in the dim light from the oil-lamps inside.

'I reckon you should hear the message before making threats,' he said.

'And what is the message?'

Floyd smirked and lowered his tone to a menacing growl.

'Are you prepared to die?'

George opened his mouth, but before he could snap back a retort, two farmers hurried over to him. With much gesticulating and frequent nervous glances at Floyd they debated their response, speaking in low and urgent tones.

While Floyd awaited their answer, Mike risked edging a pace towards Jesse.

'When do we make our move?' he whispered from the corner of his mouth.

Jesse narrowed his eyes, clearly irritated that Mike had risked exposing them by talking at such a fraught moment.

'I need to hear more,' Jesse whispered in a harsh tone that told Mike not to speak to him again. 'Wait until Floyd's fully incriminated Nyle Adams.'

Mike nodded, then moved away before anyone noticed them talking.

At the other end of the stable George finished his debate and peeled away from the two farmers to face Floyd. From the way the two men flanked him with their arms folded and their jaws set firm, Mike reckoned it would be defiance. Sure enough, a series of quick glances passed between the farmers, which resulted in each man moving to stand before one of the newcomers.

Mike noted that at least one man faced each of Floyd's men, including himself, but most of them were armed only with crude farm implements. The same couldn't be said for the men they faced.

'We will fight until we draw our last breaths,' George said, shaking a fist over his head, 'to stop Nyle Adams running us off our land.'

Floyd snorted a harsh laugh, licking his lips as he looked around the stable, his pause ensuring that everybody was watching him.

'I wasn't interested in what you'll do to keep your land. I meant are you prepared to die in this stable . . . tonight?'

For long moments silence reigned. The only movement came from the farmer's eyes slowly moving downwards to take in the fact that each of Floyd's men was packing a gun.

'Even Nyle wouldn't order you to do that,' George said with the first hint of a tremor in his voice.

'Nyle already has and so tonight we end this, one way or the other. Either you leave here one at a time, pick up your families, and move on out, or . . . ' Floyd glanced down at his holster.

By the back wall Jesse caught Mike's

eye. He gave a nod that said he'd now heard enough. He pushed himself away from the wall as did Mike.

'Or . . . ?' George asked.

'Or the first to die will be . . . ' Floyd smirked. Then in a lightning gesture, he drew his gun and swivelled at the hip, his gun swinging round to aim at Jesse.

The marshal had only a moment to react. He still managed to draw his gun, but he was too late. Floyd's deadly shot caught him in a high blow to the chest that sent him reeling into the wall, his own shot wasting itself in the straw-strewn ground.

Mike stood frozen to the spot. Floyd's unexpected action had caught him unawares. Jesse slid down the wall to lie in a crumpled heap. He looked up at him, his expression a cryptic mixture of pain, accusation and perhaps even disgust.

'Shouldn't have listened to Simmons,' he murmured, his voice fading.

As he twitched, then stilled, gunfire erupted in the stable.

Mike shook off his shock and swirled round to find himself facing an irate farmer thrusting a pitchfork at his chest.

Mike jumped to the side, arching his back, his quick motion letting him avoid the prongs, which whistled past his side and stuck into the wall behind him. The farmer had to tug to remove the tool and that gave Mike enough time to slap both hands down on his straining arms and knock him forward. Then a chop to the back of the neck sent him to his knees.

Mike turned and walked into a second farmer who launched himself at him. His outstretched arms grabbed him around the chest and both men went down. Pinned to the ground, he struggled to throw off the burly man as more gunfire exploded accompanied by cries of pain and bodies hitting the dirt.

As pandemonium reigned, proving he'd lost his chance to stop a disaster before it happened, Mike slapped his hands on the man's shoulders. He shoved while twisting and he managed to throw the man to the side, but with their arms being entangled they ended up rolling over each other.

When they came to a halt the farmer again had the upper hand. He threw a punch at Mike's face that thudded into his cheek. With the man being so close to him it landed without much force, but then his assailant raised himself slightly and jerked his head downwards.

Mike saw the blow coming. He turned his head so that the attempted head-butt only grazed his forehead, but it was strong enough to daze him.

As his vision swirled, gunfire cracked close by and an agonized cry rang out. He focused on the man pinning him down. He saw his pained grimace before he slumped down to lie on top of him.

Mike pushed the man aside and got to his feet to survey the situation.

Around the stable gunsmoke swirled in eddies. The only men left standing were himself, Floyd, and Floyd's other four men. As for the farmers, every one of them lay on the ground, bloodied repeatedly before even one of them had managed to mount an effective defence.

His disgust in his failure to stop this massacre became so strong that bile rose in his throat. Even Floyd's men stood in shocked silence as the realization sank in that they had killed a dozen men in less than a minute.

'Any alive?' Floyd asked.

To give himself time to consider his next actions Mike took that duty. He checked on each man, hoping he'd find someone alive, and resolving that if he did he'd keep the discovery a secret, but every man he checked on was dead. He was kneeling beside the last man when a cry of triumph sounded.

'You were right,' one of the hired guns, Henry Pope, said, standing back from Jesse's body. In his raised hand he was clutching a badge. 'He was a US marshal, just like Clyde said.'

Mike jerked his head up to see that everyone was looking at him.

'Jesse was a lawman?' Mike repeated in disgust. 'He used me, the damn varmint.'

Floyd sized him up, then shrugged with a gesture that appeared to say he was postponing any concerns he had about him for a while. He turned back to the dead lawman.

'Name?' he asked.

Henry rummaged through Jesse's jacket then looked up.

'He was Marshal Jesse Cole.'

'I've heard of him. Nyle should be pleased we eliminated him.'

'Or not. If a marshal was trying to get us, that means other lawmen are sure to follow.'

'Agreed. Take his body back to the ranch but leave the others here as a message to their families that it's time for them to move on out.'

While they carried out his order, Mike checked on the last man, confirming he was dead. Feeling unnaturally tired, he stood, keeping his hand close to the gun he'd not even drawn, and waited for the moment of his inevitable exposure. But they raised Jesse's body without looking at him.

So Mike moved over to join them. His movement let him feel the comforting weight in his pocket of the badge he'd owned for only a few days, which proclaimed he was a deputy marshal.

This reminder of his duty made Mike stand tall. Then he followed the men outside.

3

'So it was Marshal Jesse Cole,' Nyle Adams said, 'after all. I wonder what his plan was?'

'I reckon,' Floyd Kelly said, 'he was aiming to arrest us when he was sure what we were doing, then serve a warrant on you.'

Floyd held out the folded sheaf of papers he'd claimed from Jesse's body. While Nyle read them Mike did his best to merge into the background with the rest of the hired guns.

They had gone to Nyle Adams's sprawling ranch house; this was the first time Mike had seen it. He had already noticed that it was a prosperous ranch with a well-maintained set of buildings which were in stark contrast to the rude town in which the humble farmers had been massacred.

Unfortunately the spread was so

large that Nyle needed plenty of ranch hands, all presumably accepting of his methods, so any attempt to arrest him would be sure to end quickly and disastrously.

Nyle expressed the same view with his contemptuous flick of the wrist that consigned the warrant to the fire.

'Nobody serves a warrant on me and lives,' he muttered.

'This one sure didn't,' Floyd said. 'But more lawmen will follow.'

'They will.' Nyle gestured for Floyd to follow him to a door where he stopped and looked at the rest of the men. 'But you men did well. You don't need to worry about my problems tonight. You've earned the hospitality I've laid on.'

Nyle clicked his fingers and Floyd opened the door to reveal two women, who sashayed into the room with bottles of whiskey held aloft in both hands. The men uttered hollers of delight, all thoughts of future problems leaving their minds.

Mike made sure that he smiled too as Nyle left them to enjoy themselves. He joined in the ribald joshing as the hospitality was passed around. Then he sat at a table and nursed a whiskey.

From under a lowered hat he weighed up the situation as he watched his unwished-for colleagues paw the women. He judged that despite being the main player in the massacre Floyd had no power in the arrangements here beyond that provided by his gun.

He gravitated towards Floyd to root for information, but Floyd looked at him in the same doubtful way that he had used earlier.

'What will Nyle do now?' Mike asked.

The question made Floyd's right eye twitch before he masked it by filling up Mike's glass.

'That's no concern of yours. Your role is to do as you're told.'

The door through which Nyle had left opened and two men entered. Floyd nodded to them.

Mike avoided showing that he had seen this, but from the corner of his eye he saw that one of the men stopped beside the door. The other man moved over to one of the gunslingers, Henry, and whispered something to him.

Ribald laughter rang out, after which Henry and the woman who had been sitting on his knee left the room accompanied by more laughter. This encouraged the other woman to lead the man who had been monopolizing her attention, Walter, from the room, leaving the remaining men to sit and drink.

There was nothing obviously sinister about these movements except for the fact that Floyd appeared to have instigated them. Mike couldn't shake off the apprehensive feeling that something was amiss.

Mike considered his glass, then placed it down on the table.

'I reckon I'll keep a clear head.' He moved to go as the man by the door caught Floyd's eye and gave a brief nod. From beyond the closed door the sounds of shuffling feet came.

'Where are you going?' Floyd asked, halting him.

'I have a feeling in my bones that trouble's brewing. I trust my bones. There's enough men here to deal with it if it comes this way, so I'll scout around and see what I can see.'

'Stay and enjoy the drink and hospitality instead,' Floyd said, his tone becoming more strident. 'Besides, Nyle's already considered that problem and dealt with it. He has other men out there scouting around.'

'Then I'll help them.'

'Don't go!' Floyd snapped, raising a hand and his voice, and creating sudden quiet in the room.

'Why?'

Floyd considered him, then shrugged and continued in a softer voice.

'No reason. Leave, and the best of luck.'

Floyd smiled with a hint of something left unsaid, but Mike didn't react and turned away. On the way to the outside door he heard rustling behind him and caught movement from the corner of his eye, so he veered away to join his two associates.

He stopped and murmured his intention to scout around. They greeted the news with bored indifference, but when he left them the detour let him walk to the door at an angle that kept everyone in the room in his view.

He had taken three paces when a gunshot blasted, the sound coming from elsewhere in the ranch and echoing. Mike had already been prepared for something like this to happen and he drew his gun then backed away to the wall.

His two associates leapt to their feet and joined him as more gunfire sounded, this time coming rapidly from different directions, implying that more than one man was involved.

Then fast footfalls approached in the corridor and the door flew open to reveal Nyle Adams. He paced into the room, followed by a line of ten ranch hands. Each man had a drawn gun, and the last man to enter was holding his bloodied upper arm.

'What happened?' Mike asked.

'Henry and Walter are dead,' Nyle said in a matter-of-fact manner.

A glance at the line of grim-faced and gun-toting men answered one question, so Mike asked the other.

'Why?'

'Those gunslingers killed twelve farmers. As my activities have already interested a US marshal, more lawmen will investigate and I reckon I'll avoid another warrant when they find out that a law-abiding person such as myself has dealt with the men responsible.'

Nyle glanced at Floyd and smirked.

'And I reckon,' Floyd said, 'that three more bodies will convince any doubters.'

Floyd raised a hand, the silent order making the line of gunmen swing their guns towards Mike and his two associates.

Mike had already prepared himself for that order. With calm speed he sprayed gunfire across the line of men.

Four crisp shots rang out, each finding its target and sending guns flying away from hands. Then Mike dived to the floor to avoid the returned gunfire as the rest of the men sought their targets.

As he hit the floor, gunfire erupted and the two other men went staggering away, their chests holed before they'd even managed to fight back. Mike put them from his mind and scrambled into hiding behind the only available cover, a chair.

Bullets tore into the wood and upholstery sending splinters flying. The wood was solid enough to keep him safe, but not for long.

He didn't have the time to reload so he picked up the chair. Then with it held up as a shield he ran sideways to the door.

More gunfire tore into the wood but it was deflected away, making Floyd shout out orders for the men to outflank him. One man edged into view. Mike fired at him, but as he was using the palm of his hand to balance the chair, for one of the few times in his life the bullet flew wide of its target.

Then he reached the door.

He looked down to see that the door, with its warped base, was slightly ajar, so he looped a heel around the side. He prised the door open as another round of gunfire tore into the chair and door, this time from closer to and blasting holes in the woodwork.

He had been lucky that no bullets had pierced his shield, but that luck couldn't hold out for long. So he hurled the chair at his assailants. It flew towards the centre of the line of men, making them jump aside to avoid it, but before it reached them, Mike had kicked the door the rest of the way open and leapt through.

He jerked to the side and threw himself to the porch, the action saving him from a burst of gunfire that tore through the open doorway. He hit the wood on his side then kept the movement going to roll over a shoulder and come to his feet on the run.

Thankfully not much light was spilling out from the ranch door and windows and the half-moon was scudding behind clouds so that by the time his pursuers had reached the door he had already gained the shadows. He stayed close to the ranch wall, avoiding running across open ground and giving them an obvious target.

Only when he reached the corner did he dare to hope that he might escape.

'Spread out!' Floyd shouted from the doorway.

'He knows the truth,' Nyle added. 'Don't let him get away.'

Mike slipped around the corner then headed to the next corner. When he reached the back of the ranch house he saw more men spilling out through a back door, although they were shouting to each other in a confused manner that suggested they didn't know what had happened.

Three men looked towards Mike's position: they couldn't help but see him. Even if he reloaded he couldn't defend himself against so many men, so he anticipated his discovery and stepped out from the ranch wall.

'He went that way,' he shouted, pointing. 'He's the only one to get away. It's a hundred dollars to whoever gets him and that man's me.'

With that cry of bravado he ran for the corral, waving overhead and hollering for everyone to follow him. Some men followed while others looked around for the escapee, aiming to collect the reward for themselves.

At every pace Mike expected that someone would discover his unsubtle subterfuge and cut him down, but so many men were chasing around and adding to the chaos that he reached the fence without being challenged.

He vaulted the fence then avoided wasting time in attempting to locate his own horse. He picked a calm-looking bay, then mounted up and headed for the gate. Two men even held it open for him as others reached their horses and made ready for the pursuit.

When he'd ridden through the gate Mike looked to the ranch and saw that Floyd Kelly was in view directing operations while Nyle Adams stood quietly behind him.

Mike took a last look at Nyle, committing the sight to memory and vowing that he would return and ensure that the rancher's plan to heap all the blame for the massacre on the gunslingers failed. Then he moved to leave, but with the other riders still milling around, his movement caught Floyd's attention.

For long moments they looked at each other over fifty yards of ground. Then Mike swung his horse away and galloped to the ranch gates.

'That's Mike,' Floyd shouted from behind him. 'Kill him!'

4

They were gaining on him.

After leaving the ranch Mike had sought a route to higher ground beside the river that encircled Harmony, hoping to find a refuge, but his pursuers kept him in view at all times. Worse, the moon had now emerged from behind the clouds and was providing sufficient light to ensure there were no convenient dark spots into which he could slip.

To his right the ground sloped upwards steeply while to his left was the river, which appeared as a cold uninviting mass in the moonlight.

At the next bend he looked over his shoulder, to see that the chasing riders were fifty yards back. Their harsh shouts of encouragement came to him over the pounding of his horse's hoofs.

They were so close he could count

the individual riders. Floyd Kelly was leading a group of ten men. Other riders were further back in the gloom.

He turned to the front and concentrated on riding, but he didn't dare seek more speed for fear of becoming unseated over the unfamiliar terrain.

He followed the contours of the river, gradually getting to higher ground. With it being unlikely that he'd be able to outrun his pursuers he continued to look for a potential hiding-place, but he saw nothing.

The shouting from behind became louder, but he consoled himself with the thought that they hadn't shot at him yet, although he still thought it unlikely that they'd try to take him alive.

When he next moved around a bend in the river he looked back and saw that the riders were still fifty yards away. They hadn't closed on him. This surprised him, until the uncomfortable thought came that there was probably a reason why they weren't seeking to overpower him.

To his dismay he soon saw that he was right.

Ahead the river surged towards him through a gorge. On either side of the water there was an almost sheer stretch of rockface that was too steep for his horse to climb.

He was trapped.

He rode on, desperately looking for an alternative direction to go. He couldn't see one, but he did see that away from the river the rockface was steep for around thirty feet before it levelled off somewhat.

That observation didn't help him, so he looked at the river and considered riding into it. But with so many boulders protruding from the water, the white foam and the roaring water said that if he attempted it he'd be swept away to his death.

He would have to abandon his horse. So, there no longer being any need to conserve its strength, he galloped on, getting one last burst of speed. He aimed for the most pitted and therefore perhaps most climbable stretch of the gorge, then drew up quickly and jumped down.

He hit the ground on the run and bounded to the rock. Then without looking back he began climbing.

He thrust up hand over hand, dragging himself off the ground then upwards, all the time expecting a bullet in the back. When it didn't come, he risked a glance over his shoulder. The riders were coming to a halt at the base of the gorge, his burst of speed having bought him a few moments of precious time.

Everyone dismounted in a hurry, then the orders ripped out. From amongst the shouting Floyd's voice cried out clearly.

'Shoot him!'

Mike gritted his teeth as the first round of lead tore into the rockface, spraying splinters. He abandoned all caution and launched himself higher, grasping hold of thin handholds, kicking downwards against ledges that crumbled to dust.

With a scrambling desperation he continued to get higher.

Another volley ripped out, but as he gradually got himself away from the men this assault was no more accurate than the previous one. Then he saw that above him the slope flattened off. With a relieved leap he thrust his chest over the ledge and rolled from view.

He lay on his front, catching his breath and enjoying the respite. Then he took stock of his situation. He looked up, seeing that the gorge rose above him for another hundred feet, the terrain being climbable with ease, if he wasn't been shot at.

So he decided to use the advantage of his cover. He drew his gun, wormed his way to the edge and looked down.

The men had gone.

Mike flinched, the sight bemusing him. He had been lying on the ledge for only a few seconds and yet, aside from the milling horses, there was no movement down below.

He craned his neck, looking along the gorge, and caught glimpses of the men. They were all climbing, taking routes to his left or closer to the river. He could pin some of them down, but he judged that he was unlikely to stop someone reaching a position that was higher than his own and turning the tables on him. So he got to his feet and climbed.

Over the less steep terrain the climbing was easier than before. That let him glance down to see how the pursuers were faring, but they were all taking routes that kept them out of his view.

An eerie quietness accompanied his progress, punctuated only by his breathing and the scrape of his boots against rock. He'd judged the height well and after around a hundred feet he came out on a flat area.

Spindly pines were dotted around, masking for how far the flat area continued. He made for the trees and once he was amongst them he relaxed, enjoying the extra cover they gave him.

61

However, with the canopy above making the light level drop he couldn't see the ground.

Roots caught at his boots and toppled him. Thin dead branches that he couldn't see whipped at his face. So by the time he reached an area where the ground was too stony even for these thin trees, he was grateful to be out in the open again.

He was now closer to the roaring river. Ahead the ground rose before disappearing into a solid mass of trees. Despite the difficulty of making his way through a forest in the dark he ran towards it.

A gunshot tore at the ground at his feet, then a second whistled past his head.

He ducked and continued running, but a third shot tore out. The last shot was wilder than the others had been, but this time he saw the shooter. He was standing ahead of him, in front of the trees. And he wasn't alone.

A line of men joined him, having

clearly used their knowledge of the area to get ahead of him. With his assailants outnumbering him, he kept his gun holstered and backed away into the sparser trees behind him. Several rapid gunshots hurried him on his way, each tearing bark away.

When he reached the trees he had no respite. Figures were moving between the trunks, scurrying from one tree to the next as they closed on him. This time he loosed off a couple of shots that made his pursuers scramble into hiding. Then he turned on his heel and ran.

With men being out in the clearing and in the trees he could go in only one direction and that was towards the river. The roaring from the water echoed in his ears and he peered ahead, being unsure where the gorge started in the poor light.

An increase in the light level warned him of his impending arrival at the edge. Ten strides later he emerged from between the last two trees to find he was on the edge of the gorge. He looked down, seeing the formidable mass of the river below. Then he looked along the top of the gorge.

A thin path skirted the rim, going in both directions, but with men being ahead of him in an area he didn't know and men closing in the trees behind him he chose the less risky option and doubled back.

He ran as fast as he dared along the rim while avoiding looking down. Close by men were shouting to each other, but he put them from his mind and concentrated on landing his feet on solid rock.

He received a welcome breather from his nerve-racking progress when a ledge appeared ahead. He veered on to it, enjoying not having to teeter along with a sheer drop to his side. Then a gunshot echoed, catching a dangling sleeve.

Mike dropped to one knee and swivelled. He picked out the man coming out of the trees. With a single shot he nicked the man's arm.

The man cried out, then slipped and tumbled away.

A second man stepped up to take a bead on him. He regretted his action when the urgency of the situation made Mike pin his shoulder, the blow making him spin into a tree where he stood propped up before he slid down it to lie on his side.

Two more men emerged from the trees, but then darted back into hiding, not risking taking him on.

Feeling confident about his situation for the first time Mike waited, keeping his gun aimed at the trees and waiting for the first person to risk emerging.

Long moments passed. Then a footfall sounded behind him.

Mike swung round, but he was already too late. A man ran into him and knocked him to the ground. His gun flew from his grasp.

Mike just had enough time to register that it was Floyd Kelly and that the cautious men had been directing his attention to the trees to distract him before Floyd grabbed his collar. He yanked him up to his feet, then delivered a pile-driving punch to the jaw that sent him sprawling.

On his back Mike shook himself, then he was bodily lifted off the ground. Floyd treated him to another blow that sent him stumbling backwards.

His staggering progress let him see behind him and he realized that he was wheeling towards the edge of the gorge. Frantically he stuck out a leg and saved himself from slipping over the edge.

He teetered for a moment, then rocked forward, but his back foot was on loose ground and it slipped over the side, sending him to his knees. With one leg dangling in the air he clawed at the rock and managed to roll over to lie on the ledge. Then he moved to get up, but Floyd was already on him.

His assailant slapped both hands on his shoulders then drew him to his feet.

'Your life ends here,' Floyd said,

grinning, his teeth bright in the moonlight.

Mike looked over Floyd's shoulder and saw that the rest of the men were now on the ledge, spreading out to block his escape routes.

'You and Nyle will never get away with this,' he said.

'We already have.' Floyd pushed Mike backwards so that his heels slipped over the edge and he had to stand on tiptoes to avoid toppling over. 'But before you die, tell me who you really are. Are you another lawman or are you an arrogant young gunslinger like you claimed?'

Mike consoled himself with the thought that if Nyle was unsure of the forces that were aligned against him, he might not enjoy his victory so much.

'You'll find out, one day soon.'

Floyd snorted. 'I want the answer now. Talk and I'll throw you to your death. Say nothing and I'll keep you alive for so long you'll regret not taking the easy option.'

Mike's right foot slipped and he had to jerk it to the side to find solid ground. The action let him look down and see the river 200 feet below, thundering by and promising a quick death. He shrugged then grabbed hold of Floyd's jacket.

'I choose the third option!' he shouted.

With that promise he kicked backwards. His feet landed on air. He fell. His weight and his hold of Floyd's jacket dragged the gunslinger with him and the two men toppled over the edge.

A pained cry tore from Floyd's lips, but then Mike had problems of his own to worry about. He fought his way clear of Floyd's grip, then straightened, forcing himself to keep upright and so go into the water feet first, assuming that that would give him the best chance of survival.

He whipped through the air, the coldness of the night giving him a foretaste of the water to come.

He thought he should have reached

the water by now: the drop was longer than he'd expected, and for a frozen moment his stomach lurched with panic and he felt as if he could fall for ever.

Then he hit the water.

The river felt as if it were solid ground and his legs seemed to be being driven up through his body. But the coldness of the water tore away the pain and made him gasp. The deep breath he'd taken on the way down burst from his mouth and water rushed in filling his mouth and nose. And he still felt as if he was rushing downwards.

He waved his arms seeking buoyancy, yet he still hurtled towards the river bottom. He tried to fight off the mounting panic but with water in his mouth and no air in his lungs he failed. Frantically he thrashed back and forth trying to reverse his downward move-ment.

Suddenly he emerged from the water gasping and fighting for air. He drew in a grateful gulp, then closed his mouth before he again went under.

This time he kept calm and took stock of his situation. Experimentally he kicked out his legs and found to his relief that his limbs worked. Then with firm strokes he forced himself above the surface.

The sides of the gorge towered above him and even when he strained his neck to look backwards he couldn't see the ledge from which he'd leapt. He judged this as being good news because if he couldn't see his pursuers, they wouldn't be able to see him . . .

Then with a shock he remembered Floyd.

He thrashed around on the spot, looking out for him, but in the rushing water he couldn't see him. So he turned his attention to the river, searching for what was ahead from his low angle.

Something snagged his ankle, jerking him backwards in the water and dragging him under.

Thinking he'd been caught by vegetation, Mike kicked out, but the grip tightened and when he swung round in the water a large dark shape loomed over him.

Then the grip on his ankles was let go and hands were at his throat, tightening and pressing. Through the moiling water he looked into the face of the grimacing Floyd, straining to press his neck more tightly.

Mike chopped both hands into the man's face, but the blows landed without much force. Then both men burst on to the surface.

Mike inhaled, but Floyd had gripped his windpipe so firmly he could gasp in only a reedy whine of air. Then even that closed off as Floyd strained harder.

He had seconds to get his assailant's hands from his neck or die.

In desperation he slapped his hands on Floyd's shoulders. His failing strength wouldn't provide him with enough pressure to push him away, but the grip let him steady himself in the water.

He jerked forward, slamming his forehead against Floyd's face. It crashed into his nose with a satisfying crunch, making him throw his hands to his face.

Air rushed into Mike's lungs and he gulped it down in relief. He tried to kick himself through the water to get away from his assailant, but in the fast-flowing river he could only tread water.

Floyd shook himself. Drops of blood flew. Then he launched himself at Mike. He had the same trouble as Mike had in moving himself, and his shove merely nudged him against Mike's chest and gave Mike enough time to wrap his arms around him.

They struggled, each man trying to push the other beneath the water, but neither man could get the upper hand. Instead they just turned on the spot. Slowly Mike moved until he was looking downriver.

Ahead a large boulder was standing proud of the water, dark and ominous in the moonlight. They were heading straight for it and they couldn't avoid it.

The shock must have registered on

Mike's face as Floyd released his grip and looked over his shoulder to see the rock looming above them.

As a cry of alarm tore from his lips Floyd hit the boulder, the fast current slamming his back against the rock with bone-crunching velocity. He took the brunt of the blow but Mike still slapped into the boulder head first.

The blow rattled his teeth. Nausea overcame him.

He slipped under the water, feeling numb and giddy and unable to summon the energy to fight his way to the surface.

Darkness surrounded him. The wild but muffled sounds of the river echoed in his ears.

He waved his arms without much hope, feeling consciousness slip away, but curiously finding that he wasn't worried.

He sank lower and lower.

The darkness welcomed him.

Slowly he came to rest, feeling the river bottom pressed against his back.

The tug of the current no longer moved him and he was able to lie quietly.

Without concern he let his mouth fall open to let the water be his last breath. But instead he rasped in a long breath of air.

A distracted part of his mind told him this was an odd thing to have happened, but then the shaking started. His shoulders were gripped tightly and he spewed out a vast torrent of water.

He choked, and without control of his body he rolled on to his side to press his cheek to the rough ground. He spat out wave after wave of water, each gasp interspersed with pained intakes of breath.

At last the spasms ended and he lay on his chest, breathing shallowly.

'Just rest,' a kindly voice said.

Mike blinked rapidly. That cleared his vision and let him discern more details. He wasn't in the water any more. He was lying on the ground beside the river. People were talking near by and sparks of lights from raised brands were all around him.

He rolled on to his back to look up into the face of a man who was leaning over him. He had seen this man before, but in his confused state he couldn't place where.

'Who are you?' he gasped.

'A friend,' the man said, smiling.

5

Mike was being shaken again.

A fading nightmare of his ordeal in the water swirled through his mind, making him feel cold and wet. He tried to shrug the feeling away, but he couldn't, so he forced open his eyes. With a sigh of relief he saw that he wasn't beside the water: he was alone in a room and it was light.

He tried to sit up, but solid bands encased him from head to toe ensuring that he couldn't move. A burst of panic made his heart race, but then he saw that he was immobile only because he was wrapped in blankets. He relaxed and took stock of his situation.

His memory of recent events was fragmentary, but he remembered trying to sleep while people had moved him. Despite the interruptions, he judged those people to have acted for his benefit. Now he was lying in bed in a small room but he still felt as if he were being shaken.

The interior was only slightly larger than the bed. Strapped around the walls were crates and boxes, along with a few items of furniture. He considered the walls and with a sudden change of perspective he realized that he was in a wooden wagon and that it was the wagon that was moving.

There wasn't much room in which to move around, even if he were to get out of the bed, and there were no gaps in the wood or windows to let him look outside, but he was comfortable. So he shuffled down on the bed and settled for being gently rocked.

He dozed. When he awoke the movement had stopped. The light level was lower and from near by he heard chattering.

'Hey,' he said, his voice emerging as a croak. He coughed and, as his throat cleared, he tried again, this time louder. 'Hey, what's happening out there?'

The conversation outside stopped. Then the door opened to reveal his saviour. Again the man looked familiar but, in Mike's weak state, he couldn't figure out where he'd seen him before.

'What's happening,' the man said, 'is you're resting until you feel better.'

Mike shrugged beneath his blankets. 'Does that mean I'm supposed to feel unwell, then?'

The man laughed as he stepped up into the doorway.

'When we dragged you out of the water you were so cold we thought you dead. But you started breathing. None of us is a sawbones, but after being half-drowned we thought it best to get you warmed up and rested.'

Mike nodded, the motion making him yawn. Sleep felt deliciously close.

'I'd welcome a name,' he said, stifling another yawn.

'I am the legendary Brandon Webb,' the man said with a short bow and a smile on his lips.

Mike smiled, realizing he'd washed

up beside the show that had been in Harmony yesterday. He searched Brandon's eyes, looking for a hint that he recognized him or that he knew of the tragedy that had taken place there, but he saw only concern for his well-being.

'And where are you going, Brandon?' he asked.

'We roam wherever the fancy takes us.' Brandon moved to leave with a flourish of his long jacket. 'But you can rest assured that you could not have been luckier. You're now in the safe hands of Brandon Webb's Wild West Show, the greatest show in all the world!'

★   ★   ★

Wrapped in a blanket and enjoying the night air, Mike supped his broth.

His new companions were milling around the fire within a circle of six wagons. They were chatting animatedly while flashing warm smiles at him that let him know he was welcome to talk with them, but Mike now accepted he'd been lucky.

So, although he enjoyed seeing and hearing everyone's easy camaraderie, he took the opportunity to conserve his strength and limited himself to returning friendly nods and smiles.

He still found it hard to stay awake. He reckoned that was due to the still-tender bruise he'd received when his forehead had hit the boulder that had brought about Floyd's demise.

With his delicate state and the fact that this was the first time he'd eaten in a while, he spooned the food in slowly. When the warmth slipped down to his empty stomach he reckoned he could feel himself grow stronger.

Ten people were in Brandon's entourage. They were all busy and even if he hadn't seen some of the show before, it was obvious what most of them did.

Dexter and Sheridan were practising roping skills by lassoing a stake they'd driven into the ground while the riders Logan and Clifford were caring for the horses with devoted attention.

The Cheyenne performers, Big Man and Little Feather, who kept themselves apart from the group in a way that made them appear a real couple, had laid out their knives and tomahawk for sharpening. Despite their names, they had drawling Southern accents.

The sharpshooter Victor Clancy was oiling a gun with the intense concentration of someone who relied upon it. He was one of the few people not to smile at Mike; he was the brother of Eve, the singer, who often trilled to herself. Eve, whom he judged to be the youngest and about his own age, had a pleasing oval face and black hair that cascaded down her back. She flicked it whenever she looked at him.

Unlike the others, who looked at him openly, she acted discreetly as if she didn't want to be noticed. Later, when she spoke to her brother, he scowled at her and snapped back a harsh retort that made her frown and stop looking his way.

The performers who most aroused his curiosity were the ones he hadn't seen perform: the dancers Lula and Belle. These women talked and giggled excitedly. They were enticingly attractive and graceful, and they walked with skipping paces along with much twirling of skirts.

He watched them from the corner of his eye and noted that nobody else was paying them attention, so he presumed that this was their normal behaviour.

'Interesting, eh?' Brandon said, coming over to sit with him.

Mike coughed in embarrassment at being caught looking at the women.

'You're *all* interesting.'

Brandon leaned towards him and winked. 'That's what we're paid to be.'

'And where will you be paid next?'

'Ah, payment. That would be nice. Recently we performed to some home-steaders in Harmony. Nice people, but shockingly poor and our performance was rudely curtailed. Do you know the place?'

The sobering thought of how the farmers' delight at watching this show had turned to tragedy made Mike frown. But he didn't want to put Brandon at risk from Nyle Adams's ire by making him aware of those events.

'I do,' he said.

'So we're seeking out richer pickings. In two days we're performing in Redemption City. Then we'll move on further west.'

This direction would take him away from Harmony, but bearing in mind his weak state, for the moment that felt the right way to go.

'I can't pay you for your kindness. I lost everything in the water except for the clothes I'm wearing.'

Brandon spread his hand and shrugged, as if the thought of payment had never occurred to him.

'Your recovery will be payment enough.' He coughed and cast a guarded look at Mike. 'But was there anything in particular you wish you hadn't lost?'

Mike wondered whether he was referring to his deputy marshal's badge, which he no longer had, but Brandon's questioning glance at his empty holster suggested otherwise.

'I'm not trouble, if that's what you mean.' He nodded at Dexter and Sheridan. 'They're armed too.'

'They need to be to keep away the trouble we sometimes encounter out on the trail.'

Mike considered revealing his own status, to put Brandon's mind at rest, but he wasn't sure what his status was. He'd been deputized for a specific mission, which he'd failed to complete, and until he could rectify that situation he didn't think he could claim to be Sheriff Simmons's deputy either.

'And that's the only reason I was packing a gun too. And if it's all the same with you, I'll stay with you until you reach Redemption City, then move on.'

Brandon's furrowed brow suggested he was considering asking him more questions, not the least of which would be how he came to be in the river. Mike didn't think he could devise a suitable answer but, thankfully, Brandon nodded and stood.

'As you wish,' he said.

★ ★ ★

On his second day with Brandon's show Mike felt stronger.

His head was still sore, but although he didn't feel a need to wrap himself in blankets and sleep, he still rode inside Brandon's wagon. With nothing else to occupy his mind he planned his return to Harmony.

He decided that Nyle Adams would presume him dead and so he wouldn't send anyone after him. That meant he could return unexpectedly and bring Nyle to justice. Without money, getting back to Harmony would be difficult, but he figured that continuing to be 'dead' was worth the trouble.

The next day he'd shaken off the

ill-effects of his ordeal. So he rode up front on Brandon's wagon, where he enjoyed his tall tales of the delights on offer in his show and his even taller tales of his travels.

By the time they arrived at Redemption City, Mike had resolved to see the full show before he left. Although even if, after Brandon's tales, it proved to be the most remarkable thing he'd ever seen, it would be a disappointment.

Brandon headed into the largest saloon. After negotiating with the owner, Kurt Rogers, he emerged, beckoned the wagons to draw up before the saloon and ordered everyone to set up the show. In his brief time inside the saloon he had even located the leader of a supply convoy, Billy Grant, who was heading east and who would let Mike work his passage.

To show his thanks Mike tried to help with the setting up of the show, but quickly he had to accept he was in the way. So he offered to get the message out that they were in town, but

Brandon had already given that task to the women.

When they donned skirts that Mike viewed as indecently short, and which Brandon viewed as essential, he decided to tag along to make sure no potential spectators became too frisky.

He walked beside them as they headed down the road. They attracted the kind of interest he had expected, with catcalls and whistles aplenty. Eve took the lead and to every man who stopped to appraise them, she passed on the message that they should come to the saloon at sundown, something everybody readily agreed to do.

Most of the attention was good-natured, but when they'd reached the end of the road and started working their way back, the trouble that Mike had worried about arrived.

Two men were talking outside the stable, but the approaching women made them peel away from the wall.

'Now what are you pretty ladies doing?' one man asked.

'Come to the saloon at sundown,' Eve said with a wink, 'and you'll find out.'

'That's a long time to wait. I might not be around then. Show me now.'

'No free shows.' She waggled a finger.

'I'd don't need no free show. I'd surely pay for an hour with you.'

Despite the rude presumption of what they did, Eve responded with a raised and enticing eyebrow that suggested the tantalizing prospect that she might take him up on that offer.

Then with a giggle she moved off. The man shot out a hand and grabbed her arm, then swung her around to hold her against his chest.

'What do you charge?' he demanded.

To Mike's way of thinking, that was one insult too many. He paced up to them.

'Let her go,' he said, keeping his tone pleasant.

The man and his companion swung their gazes round to consider him.

'Now why should I do that?'

'Because — '

'Because if you don't,' Eve said, 'I won't be able to entertain you tonight.'

The man kept his hand clamped on her arm as he considered Mike, then sneered.

'And will he be there tonight?'

'It'll just be you, me . . . and a few hundred more.' She licked her lips. 'But you'll be the one I sing to.'

She offered him a huge smile. After he'd cast a glance at his companion, with an aggrieved snap of the wrist he released his hold.

'I'll see you there.'

Eve fluffed her hair, still smiling, then breezed away down the boardwalk, closely followed by the other women. Mike loitered to make sure the surly men didn't follow, then hurried on to catch up with Eve before she reached the next group of men who were standing outside a mercantile.

She cast him a bemused look. 'Will you continue to protect us until we get back to the wagons, then?'

'Don't worry,' he said, eyeing the two nearest men for signs of trouble. 'I'll stay vigilant.'

'I was worried you'd say that.'

Mike had hoped to be thanked, so this comment made him flinch back.

'If I hadn't have stepped in, you could have faced a whole heap of trouble.'

'We could have, but the trouble would have happened *only* because you stepped in.' She stopped and set her hands on her hips. 'Did you not consider that we've been to a hundred towns and dealt with a thousand men like them?'

'I guess you have. I'm . . . ' He trailed off. The next men the women would approach had yet to look their way, but something about them drew his attention.

'Don't be annoyed,' Eve said, a smile replacing her stern attitude. 'I am grateful and I'll miss having a handsome stranger like you in our midst.'

Despite the compliment Mike continued to stare at the men, wondering why they made him feel edgy. Then a flash of recognition hit him.

It had been only a brief sighting while he'd been running to the corral at Nyle Adams's ranch, but these men were two of Nyle's ranch hands. And they were watching the crowd outside the saloon with the studied concentration of people who were looking for someone.

'If I'm only making things worse,' Mike said, while watching the ranch hands from the corner of his eye, 'I'd better leave you, then.'

'I don't want you to go,' Eve murmured, her eyes wide and shocked, but Mike ignored her and slipped into the nearest alley.

He heard her mutter to the other women about his strange behaviour before they moved on. Then he waited, his fists bunched in expectation of him having to fight for his life.

When several minutes had passed

without the ranch hands appearing and confronting him, he risked glancing out of the alley. He saw that they were still looking at the milling people.

Clearly Nyle Adams hadn't taken his death for granted and he still had men out looking for him. As Billy Grant wouldn't be leaving town until after the show, he needed to find somewhere to hole up until then. So he headed to the backs of the buildings and took a circuitous route to reach the side of the saloon.

To his relief the crowd was continuing to grow, and so he mingled in with them. He chose a spot on the edge of the boardwalk beside a corner post that afforded him some protection from being seen.

He looked for the ranch hands and anyone else who might take an unnatural interest in him, while appearing to watch the showfolk. Despite his concern, viewing them as a spectator let him see how impressive they were.

With efficient speed they built a stage

using the blue-painted wagon as a backdrop while others laid out covered stakes and objects under cloths. Their actions only added to the mystery and the sense that something exciting was about to happen.

Kurt let his bartenders serve drinks outside and by sundown the crowd was good-natured and enthused, with more people arriving by the minute.

Mike welcomed the gathering gloom and the press of people, judging that it would make it increasingly difficult for anyone to pick him out. So when Brandon stepped up on to the stage to face the audience, he allowed himself to relax enough to enjoy what was to come.

As the last rays of sunlight faded away Brandon, with an overhead gesture that called for quiet, declared the show open.

It followed the same format as the show he'd seen in Harmony. Logan and Clifford demonstrated their riding skills. Then Dexter and Sheridan lassoed, after which Big Man threw knives at Little Feather.

Darkness had arrived when the part of the show he'd looked forward to the most came, and it was so captivating it even made him feel that keeping an eye out for the ranch hands was no longer important.

Eve sang the song Floyd had interrupted in Harmony. It proved to be a tale of a lost love who had ridden off across the plains and who had not returned. This beautifully sung and heartfelt song silenced everyone.

While singing she made eye contact with many in the enthralled crowd and for one heart-stopping moment she looked at him with a wistful gaze. It was probably a coincidence that at that moment she was singing about her sadness at never being able to see her love again, but it made Mike gulp. And everyone else had been moved too, for, when she finished, she received the loudest cheer of the night.

Then the dancing girls arrived.

Accompanied by Dexter and Sheridan's jaunty banjo playing, Belle and Lula pirouetted and high-kicked. He was disappointed that Eve didn't dance, but he smiled on seeing that she chose this moment to go around the gathered crowd with a pail.

He had wondered how they earned a living when they didn't charge to see the show, but it became clear now. With a hand on her hip she flirted with the menfolk so that by the time she returned, her pail was brimming with bills and coins.

Then came the finale, which turned out to be a play set on the stage.

Eve played a rancher's wife, single-handedly running a ranch while yearning for her husband to return from an unspecified mission. Mike enjoyed the play, noting that it expanded upon her song.

The story was simple. A dastardly man played by Brandon wooed her, while explaining to the audience from the corner of his mouth his plans to kill her and then run her ranch. His plan worked well until her husband played by Victor returned and saved her by running Brandon off.

It was corny and contrived but everyone was in good spirits and they cheered at the right times. To close the story Eve sang a final song, after which Brandon whipped off his cloak to announce the greatest show of all time was over, making many people gasp on realizing that it was he.

The prolonged cheers suggested the boast wasn't altogether unfounded after which the audience disbanded in good spirits.

'That was a good show,' a voice said from behind him.

Mike flinched, realizing that for the last hour the show had transported him away from his problems and that he hadn't even thought about the men who were looking for him. Slowly he turned, then relaxed when he found he was facing the convoy leader, Billy Grant.

'It sure was,' Mike said with a sigh of relief. 'I'm glad I got the opportunity to see it, but I'm ready to go now.'

Mike cast a last lingering look at Eve, who was walking over to her brother.

'You don't look ready.'

Mike frowned. Eve and Victor were starting to argue. Victor was pointing an angry finger at her, while Eve stood with her hands on her hips. He didn't know what the problem was and with some reluctance he turned away.

'I guess I'll have to be,' he said.

Billy snorted a laugh, letting Mike know that he'd noticed where his attention had been. As they headed off, he regaled Mike with a tale of a showgirl he'd once known.

When they reached the convoy on the outskirts of town the wagons weren't ready to move out. Only the other workers were close by, so Mike helped hitch up the horses. Since not everyone who should be here had returned yet, Billy sent two men off to round them up.

By the time they were ready to leave Brandon's people had also packed up their wagons and they too were moving out.

Mike watched the wagons trundle by, going in the opposite direction, hoping to catch a last sight of Eve, but she wasn't visible. Neither did Brandon or anyone else look his way.

A twinge of irritation snapped at his mind. They'd forgotten about him quickly, but, then again, that was the life they led. They met people then moved on. He would become another tale they'd share around a campfire. Curiously, that thought made him smile and he turned away.

As he took up his position on the second wagon four riders emerged from the stable. Kurt Rogers and a bartender were riding beside the two men who had been rude to Eve earlier. They were muttering to each other and their gazes were set on the departing train of Brandon's wagons.

Their demeanour gave Mike the

impression that they were planning mischief. But he didn't have the time to both warn Brandon and leave with the convoy. And he did need to begin his journey back to Harmony.

As the convoy headed off, he sat hunched in his seat until they swung past an outlying building where he looked back. The men had now moved on into town where they'd met up with two other riders.

All six men were talking with their gazes set on Brandon's receding wagons. Then, with a firm swing of their horses, they followed the wagons out of town.

Worse, the new men were the ranch hands he'd been trying to avoid.

Mike didn't know if they had joined up with the other men because they suspected that Brandon was harbouring him, but either way, the sighting made his next decision an easy one.

Despite his desire to remain unseen, he couldn't let Brandon suffer because of his kindness. So he tipped his hat to the driver. Then he slipped to the edge of the seat and jumped down.

'Hey,' the driver shouted, 'what do you think you're doing?'

Mike said nothing as he raised a hand to ward off the dust from his eyes while the wagons trundled past. When the last wagon had passed he saw two trailing horses tethered at the back.

He ran after the horses then vaulted up on to the back of the nearer one. He righted himself before nudging the horse on to slacken the tether.

Two minutes later he was free and drawing back, but his actions hadn't gone unnoticed.

'You thieving varmint!' the driver of the last wagon shouted at him, shaking a fist.

'I'm no thief,' Mike said, waving to him. 'I'm a lawman and I'll be back.'

With that declaration cheering him, Mike swung round and hurried back to town.

6

As Mike hurried on into the night he hoped to catch sight of the riders, but they weren't visible. They should have only a few minutes' lead on him, so he wondered whether he had made a mistake about their intentions.

When he first saw Brandon's wagons he considered how he should act seeing that he wasn't sure where the following riders were, when they might attack, or even whether they really were up to no good.

Then he saw that the wagons had drawn to a halt. A commotion was in progress with people milling around.

He slowed to approach the wagons cautiously. The lead wagon stood sideways, the other five drawn up at an angle to the one in front to create a rough semicircle, perhaps in defence. Many of the showfolk had jumped down from the wagons and, facing the semicircle, were riderless horses.

A gunshot cracked out, followed by a cry of alarm.

Sure now that Brandon was in trouble Mike hurried on, peering ahead and trying to discern in the gloom what the scurrying figures were doing. Thirty yards from the wagons he jumped down from his horse and, on the run, carried on, but before he reached the semicircle someone lit a brand, throwing the scene into sharp relief.

Instantly he saw that the showfolk didn't need his help.

The men he'd seen in town had followed Brandon, after all, but Victor had fired the gunshot as a warning to Kurt Rogers, who was thrusting his arms high. Faced with an array of drawn guns, Nyle Adams's ranch hands took flight, but Dexter and Sheridan unfurled lengths of rope, twirled them over their heads, then let fly.

With deft accuracy the ropes landed over the men's heads and dragged tightly around their chests to bring them to a halt. They struggled to escape until one man was dragged on to his back, then reeled in while the other man got a second rope around his chest, the accuracy of the throw gathering a round of chortling laughter.

The bartender and another man tried to escape between the wagons, but Logan and Clifford stepped into view and with simultaneous punches to the jaw they felled the running men. The man who had grabbed Eve earlier ran away from the wagons, but he was quickly cut off by Brandon and Big Man.

The man ran one way then the other, seeking an escape route, until he found the only direction available to him, this being towards the women, who had gathered together. But when he tried to barge them aside Belle delivered a swinging kick between his legs that brought him to his knees bleating in pain. Lula pushed him over and Little Feather placed a mocking foot on his back, where she posed to another round of laughter and applause.

Mike slowed his progress to approach the wagons at a walking pace. Then he found that the only person in danger was himself, as the showfolk turned their attention and guns on the new unknown danger.

'It's me,' he said, raising his hands. 'I've come to . . . to help.'

His comment generated another burst of laughter as Brandon beckoned for him to come into the light.

Mike considered the ranch hands, wondering whether he had enough time to disappear into the shadows and remain unnoticed. But both men were already looking at him, and their narrowed eyes confirmed that he'd already lost any chance of remaining 'dead'.

'And we're grateful for your *help*,' Brandon said. He gestured at the subdued men. 'But as you can see, we've had plenty of practice at keeping our money from men like these.'

'Your money?' Kurt snorted. 'You

liar. One of your women stole a — '

'Be quiet,' Victor shouted, then let off a shot that winged past Kurt's head and made him bend over, clutching his ear.

'You shot my ear off,' he bleated.

'I only nicked it. Try anything else and I'll have 'em both.'

Kurt glanced at the blood on his palm, then fingered his torn ear while backing away.

'I hope you choke on the money,' he said.

Mike sized up the raiders. He was unsure of what everyone's motives were for joining up with the ranch hands, but Victor's accurate shooting in a fraught situation had impressed him. His admiration died when Victor turned his surly gaze on him.

'Will we ever get rid of you?' he demanded.

'Hey,' Brandon said before Mike could reply. 'He came back to help us.'

'I did,' Mike said, setting his hands on his hips. 'As you'd been kind to me, I couldn't leave town and ignore that these men were following you.'

The ranch hands glanced at each other and nodded, showing they had understood that his declaration had also been for their benefit.

'And so you insulted us with your unwanted presence again, did you?' Victor asked. He gestured at the captured men. 'As if we couldn't see off these men, but you could.'

Mike sighed, putting Victor's annoyance down to the argument he'd had back in town with Eve. That thought made him look for her, but although he judged that everyone else was outside, he couldn't see her.

He turned his back on Victor and tipped his hat to Brandon.

'I am forever in your debt,' he said.

He moved to go, but Victor snorted with derision.

'Slink off like the snake you are and if you ever come sniffing around my sister again, I'll spoil your pretty-boy face by taking more than your ears off.'

Mike came to a halt, looking away

from the wagons. Unseen by anyone he smiled, having reached a reasonable conclusion as to why Victor had such an irrational hatred for him. He had spent only a short time with Eve, but it would seem that he'd garnered a significant and welcome reaction.

Although it was unlikely that he would ever see these people again he saw no reason to put Victor's mind at rest. He swung round.

'You shouldn't be so cock-sure,' he said, speaking loudly to ensure the ranch hands also heard his warning. 'You may be able to nick a man's ear at twenty paces, but I could knock the wings off that fly buzzing over your head at forty paces.'

Victor set his feet wide apart. 'I'd like to see that.'

Victor's sneer suggested that only a show of skill would satisfy his anger and many of the showfolk murmured happily to each other, sensing enter-tainment, but Brandon raised a hand.

'If you two would stop bellowing at

each other, can someone answer me something — has anyone seen Eve?'

For several moments nobody moved as Victor and Mike continued to glare at each other. Then Victor flinched and swung round to Big Man.

'I thought she was riding with you,' he said.

When Big Man shook his head, others called out for her, but they got no response. So they searched the wagons, but she wasn't in any of them.

Worse, the last time anybody could remember seeing her was in Redemption City. This led to Victor stepping up to Kurt.

'Where is she?' he demanded.

Kurt shook his head. 'I don't know nothing about no — '

'I said,' Victor roared, slapping Kurt's face backhanded, 'what have you done with her?'

Kurt held his cheek, shaking his head. 'I don't even know which one Eve is.'

'The singer!' Victor shouted, raising his hand.

'Enough,' Brandon said, joining them. 'Kurt doesn't know where she is. I don't believe he'd kidnap her quietly then mount such an inept raid.'

Victor's glaring eyes appeared angry enough to suggest that he would continue to hit Kurt until he got an answer. But he took deep breaths while he kept his hand held back. Then he nodded and lowered his hand.

'We'll do it your way, then,' he said.

'Obliged,' Brandon said. 'We'll head back to town and see what we can find out, but we'll keep them with us in case we can't find her.'

'And you'd better hope,' Victor said, pointing at each man in turn, 'that my sister hasn't been hurt or I'll do the same to you ten times over.'

Without further discussion Brandon beckoned for everyone to return to the wagons. While Logan and Clifford each took care of two of the men Mike volunteered to bundle the ranch hands into a wagon.

He slapped a hand on each man's back to push them forward, but then used the motion to cover up his leaning in to whisper in their ears.

'How many are searching for me?' he asked.

'You'll get an answer,' one man said, 'just before you get shot to hell.'

'You're wrong. I'm the one who'll be doing the shooting. So you can send this message back to Nyle Adams. I'm alive and I'm coming to get him.'

'You won't get within fifty miles of Harmony.'

Mike reached the wagon in which they'd be secured and turned them round to face him.

'Either way, I've not told these people what happened there. That matter is between Nyle Adams and me.'

He received curt nods, acknowledging that he was the only one they had an issue with. He considered questioning them as to whether they had anything to do with Eve's disappearance, but with time pressing he pushed them up inside the wagon and went to his horse.

Within a minute they were retracing their steps back to town with the wagons in the lead and Mike bringing up the rear.

When they arrived back in town Brandon asked around. It didn't take him long to discover what had happened, not that that was hard. Everybody in town was talking about it.

Ten minutes earlier a rider had galloped through town with a woman held down over his saddle. The sight had gathered bemused interest, but the rider had swung around to parade up and down the road twice until everyone had seen that the woman was the singer from the show. Then he'd galloped out of town heading east, following on behind Billy Grant's convoy.

While Brandon and the other show-folk returned to their wagons with most of them discussing why someone should have acted so strangely, Mike hurried out of town ahead of them.

Although he didn't know whether Eve's kidnapping was connected with the ranch hands and their quest to find him, he couldn't shake off the feeling that this situation was odd. But he put those thoughts from his mind and concentrated on the task at hand.

He was unable to see far in the poor light but the sightings had been clear enough: the rider had taken the same route as the convoy. Mike was able to make out recent wheel-ruts, so he followed them.

A half-mile on he looked back and saw that Brandon's wagons were now following. They were holding up brands to light their way and they were taking the same route as he had.

Then, coming to him over the night air, he heard a distant scream.

He stopped and listened, his ear cocked to one side as he tried to work out the direction of the scream. It came again. This time he was sure it was a woman's voice and that she was shouting for help. And he could tell where it had come from.

He doubled back for a hundred yards, then hurried on towards the direction of the scream. He waved at the wagons, unsure whether they'd be able to see him, but a minute later he was relieved to see them move towards him, her scream obviously having reached them too.

'Help me!' the woman shouted.

The voice was closer than before and was clearly Eve's. He peered into the darkness and gradually discerned a sprawling pile of boulders. The sound was coming from in front of them.

He slowed, judging from her frequent cries that she wasn't in immediate danger. Sure enough, when he saw her she was sitting on the ground, trussed up. She shouted for help again, then fell silent when she saw him approach.

'It's me, Mike,' he said as he jumped down from his horse.

'Mike?' she said. 'I thought you'd left town.'

'I came back to rescue you.'

He looked along the length of the boulders, seeing nothing untoward but still being unable to dismiss the odd nature of the situation.

'I don't know where he's gone,' she said, her voice breaking with suppressed emotion. 'Untie me quickly before he comes back.'

'Don't worry. I'm here now.'

He hurried over to her and worked on the ropes that tied her hands behind her back. She had been gagged, but the gag had been tied loosely and it had fallen down to lie around her neck.

When he'd removed the last rope she leapt to her feet and threw herself into his arms.

'Thank you, thank you,' she breathed, while giving him a bone-crushing hug that warmed his heart and made him glad he'd returned.

By now the wagons were a hundred yards away, so he disentangled himself from her arms and shouted out to Brandon that he'd found Eve and that she was safe. Then he turned back to enjoy his last few moments with her before he returned to the convoy.

'Who did this?' he asked.

'I don't know. I didn't see his face. As we were getting ready to leave a man clamped a hand over my mouth and dragged me into the shadows.'

Mike gulped. 'Did he . . . ?'

'He didn't do anything but hold me. Then we saw you galloping through town after Brandon. After that he took me to his horse and paraded me around town before taking me here and tying me up.'

Mike shivered. Her emphasis on the kidnapper bringing her here only after he'd passed through town strengthened his feeling of something being very wrong.

'It's almost as if he wanted to be seen taking you,' he mused. He glanced at the wagons, which were now slowing. 'But you're safe now.'

She placed a hand on his arm and kissed his cheek. Then she moved away to wave at the wagons and call out that she was fine.

With the wet imprint of her lips burning his cheek he felt emboldened enough to head towards the boulders alone to search for any sign of where her kidnapper had gone. The lights from the wagons lit his way and threw out sharp shadows beyond the boulders.

He explored behind the largest rocks but he saw no sign of her abductor. He had disappeared as mysteriously as he'd appeared.

Mike turned and saw that Brandon and a relieved-looking Victor had surrounded her while she explained what had happened.

'What did he really want?' Mike murmured to himself as he moved to join them.

A hand slapped over his mouth while a second hand clamped itself around his chest and drew him backwards.

'You!' a voice murmured in his ear.

Mike winced as his assailant drew him backwards into the shadows. The voice, which he'd heard only a few

116

times before, provided an answer to his pondering.

The assailant removed his hand from over his mouth and replaced it with a gun, which he pressed up against his cheek.

'Floyd Kelly?' Mike asked.

'Sure,' Floyd hissed in his ear. 'You weren't the only one who avoided drowning. I got out too and followed you, waiting to get you alone. Then I saw you escorting that showgirl around town and I thought that kidnapping her would get your attention.'

Mike stared into the darkness, hearing Brandon and the others talking but not hearing any suggestion that they'd noticed his disappearance.

'And now that you've got my attention?'

'You're the only one who knows what really happened in Harmony.' Floyd shrugged. 'So you die.'

Mike heard the dismissive tone, as if there was only one possible answer. Floyd pressed the gun tightly into his cheek, grinding it against his teeth through the skin.

In desperation Mike elbowed Floyd in the guts and jerked himself away, but he was too late.

The gun roared, and the night exploded into a thousand shooting stars.

7

Fragmented visions flashed through Mike's mind. Disembodied voices flitted in and out of his hearing. Unseen people poked him.

Through it all there was the all-consuming pain in his head.

'Is he dead?' someone asked.

'He sure is,' another replied. 'Look at him. He shot off his face!'

Hands clawed at his neck. 'Wait. I don't believe it. He has a pulse.'

'Leave him be. It's kinder.'

'No!' a woman cried out.

For a timeless period darkness reigned.

Then a light shone into his eyes, brilliant light that burned deep into his brain. He struggled to get away from it, but he couldn't escape.

Someone pinned him down and tortured him by poking red-hot needles into his gums. He cried out in silent agony.

Darkness stole him again.

The light returned, brighter than before and in the middle of it a face swam in and out of focus.

'Can you do anything?' someone asked.

The question wasn't addressed to him.

'I've seen worse,' the man said, 'but only on dead men. It'll cost to try. I've got the time, if you've got the money to waste.'

Mike didn't hear the answer as his vision clouded and a pleasant dream took him away from their disturbing conversation. This was odd, as he usually awoke the moment he realized he was dreaming, but this time something told him that it would be better to stay asleep and enjoy the dream.

He was riding across a desert, which was devoid of life, heading for a distant row of monolithic outcroppings. Disconcertingly the rocks resembled jagged shards of teeth.

He rode on, somehow covering vast distances towards them, but when he came close to the nearest toothlike rock, it fell over and shattered, the moment being accompanied by a sharp pain in his mouth.

Mike leaned to the side and spat out a broken tooth. He steeled himself, not liking where this dream was heading, but he still felt unwilling to wake up.

He rode towards the second rock, but that too crumbled sending an even greater burst of pain ripping through his mouth.

He spat out another tooth and rode on, determined not to let the pain make him turn back or wake up, but every time he approached a rock it fell and crumbled. And every time the pain grew and he lost another tooth.

Before long his mouth was aflame, unable to bear the lightest touch of his questing tongue. His jaw was a ragged raw wound and hot air blew into his mouth through a hole in his cheek. But he wouldn't give in, forcing himself to approach the last three rocks.

The first crumbled and made him scream in pain.

The second shattered and sent him tumbling from his horse to writhe on the ground in agony.

Somehow he forced himself to stand and stagger on towards the very last rock.

He placed a hand to his jaw. It touched a mass of pulped meat that didn't feel as if it were his own. The hand came away drenched in blood but he forced himself to probe again, finding that most of his face wasn't even there and he could touch his tongue without entering his mouth.

He stood before the last rock and he watched it explode into fragments.

He screamed in a tormented hell. Even when he'd spat out tooth after tooth until there was nothing left in his mouth other than a yawning maw the pain still tore through his head.

Insanity clawed at his tortured mind.

He had to escape and he chose his

only option. With a wrench he forced himself to flee this dream world and awake.

The real world drove away the desert dream and the face he'd seen before swam back into view looking down at him. The man held a brutal metal object aloft that reflected the far too bright light deep into his retinas.

'I'm ready to begin now,' the man said. 'This will hurt.'

* * *

Mike opened his eyes, willing his latest desert nightmare to leave his mind.

He was lying in bed in the same wagon as he had been in when he'd recovered from his ordeal in the water.

This situation was different, but he forced himself to think that it was the same for as long as possible. For several seconds that worked, but reality intruded and told him this situation was worse, far, far worse.

He'd been shot in the head at point

blank range. By rights he should be dead. Somehow he had survived, but clearly not without suffering.

Tentatively he raised a hand to his face. He felt bandages encasing his jaw and when he rolled his eyes down he could see the tops of them.

He gulped to moisten his dry throat, hearing his breathe whistle through a hole in the bandages, but he was unwilling to move his jaw or try to speak. His lower face felt numb, as if it didn't exist, and something told him he didn't want to move his tongue, no matter how dry his mouth felt.

The wagon was still and the light level was low; but he couldn't hear anyone moving around nearby. He didn't think he could attract anyone's attention. So he whistled in a long breath for strength, then placed his hands to the bed and pushed.

He didn't move, but then he got the idea to rock himself to the side while pushing. This time he rolled over to a sitting position. His head swam and his vision blurred worryingly, but after another deep breath the room stopped its apparent movement, so he stood up.

He swayed and had to slap a hand on the wall to stop himself falling, but after he'd stood for several seconds he felt strong enough to try moving again. He looked to the door, planning his next movement.

His gaze alighted on a small mirror set into the wall above a table. He felt sure that he didn't want to see himself, but he went over to the mirror anyhow.

The sight that greeted him was as he'd imagined it. Bloodshot fevered eyes looked back at him and bandages encased his cheeks and jaw.

The bandages were clean, but what they covered he didn't like to guess. Experimentally he ran a finger along the top of the bandage covering his left cheek and it came away slightly.

Knowing he shouldn't do it, but unable to stop himself, he worked away at the bandage, loosening it. Then he saw a knife on the table. He began cutting, shedding an outer bandage, then a second, to reveal the sticky mass of a poultice.

This released a rank smell. With a contemptuous swipe he wiped away a layer of the poultice to reveal some of the face beneath.

He screamed. Pain shot through his jaw. He screamed again.

They found him writhing on the floor, whimpering sounds that wouldn't form into words until mercifully he passed out.

★   ★   ★

'Don't do that again,' Brandon said with a wink and an admonishing shake of the finger. 'We can't afford to have you stitched up again and my needlework's not a pretty sight.'

'Neither am I,' Mike said, or at least he thought it. He was able to make his tongue move, but not his jaw and the words emerged as a croaked slur of sounds.

He must have been able to convey his feelings as Brandon nodded.

'Don't worry. The doctor said he'd seen worse. And you're alive. None of us expected that when we found you.'

'What happened?'

'If you're asking who shot you, we don't know.' Brandon waited and although that wasn't what he'd meant, Mike nodded. 'We heard a shot, came over. A man was running for a horse. Victor went after him, but he got away. We didn't waste time trying to find out who he was. We ran off our prisoners and got you to someone who could help you.'

Mike snorted, picturing the scene of Victor half-heartedly chasing after Floyd.

'How bad is it?'

'I'm sorry. I can't make out what you're saying and you need to rest.' Brandon offered a tentative smile that suggested he knew what he'd been asked.

Mike couldn't summon the strength

to argue, so he lay back on the bed and willed himself to be calm and rest. But it didn't work.

The remainder of the night dragged, as did the days and nights that followed.

They'd removed the mirror and anything that reflected light in case he was tempted to look at himself again. So he could do nothing but sleep when he could at night, then try to let the gentle rocking of the wagon during the day lull him into a thoughtless fugue.

Only Eve and Brandon came to see him. She fed him and helped him with his ablutions, but she wouldn't meet his eye and she didn't talk.

Mike didn't mind her silence.

Brandon did talk, but not about anything related to his injury.

A week passed before he had his first break in the routine. They arrived in Carmon and set about putting on a show.

Brandon came in to say he was well enough to sit outside and watch if he wanted to, but even though the night air would do him good, he didn't want to face being seen, so he declined.

Brandon left, shaking his head. Outside the door a worried conversation about him took place in low tones. The conclusion to this debate came after the show when Doctor Willis visited.

The doctor set out fresh bandages from a black bag, then sat beside him on the bed and murmured words of encouragement as he removed the bandages. Mike searched his eyes and was relieved to see he didn't react unduly to the sight of his injury.

'How bad?' Mike croaked, being heartened to hear the words emerge relatively clearly and even feeling his jaw move slightly.

'I won't lie to you. It's bad and if you try any more damn fool tricks like picking at your face again, you'll die.'

'Why?'

'Fiddling with gunshot wounds invites the green blight in, if it's not in there already. If you get shot in an arm or a leg and it sets in, I can saw the limb off and save you, but if I saw your head off, you'll find it hard to breathe.'

'I guess so.'

Willis prodded around the cheeks and neck while sniffing.

'But it looks clean to me. If it was going to go bad, I reckon it would have done by now.'

'Does that mean it'll go good?'

Willis narrowed his eyes, clearly not having understood Mike's sarcastic comment, but with a shrug he assumed what he'd been asked.

'If the bullet had been angled an inch higher, it'd have shot your brains out; an inch lower, it'd have taken your jaw off. As it was, it went through your cheek.' Willis demonstrated with a finger on his own face. 'Then it cut across your mouth taking several teeth with it and tore out at an angle through your other cheek, cracking your jaw in the process.'

Mike gulped. 'Lucky.'

'You might not feel it, but you were. The wound looks mighty ugly now and you'll have two fearsome scars, but the bullet left enough skin to stitch up the cheeks and enough teeth for you to eat. You'll probably have a lop-sided jaw, but the scars will settle in with time.' He rocked his head from side to side, considering Mike's cheeks. 'And you could grow a beard. That might cover some of it.'

'But not enough to avoid scaring the ladies.'

Willis frowned. 'I can tell that you must have delighted them before, but from now on you'll have to impress them with your skill. What is it, lassoing, riding . . . ?'

'I'm not with the show. I was just visiting.'

'Well, it shouldn't affect your work. What did you do?'

'I was a law . . . ' Mike sighed. After this injury it felt as if that life were a long way behind him in time, distance and capability. 'I could shoot well.'

With his pronounced lisp the words came out poorly, making Willis furrow his brow in confusion.

'Then do that,' he still said encouragingly.

Mike nodded, then returned to his bed.

Shortly afterwards the wagons got moving. As usual they stopped a few miles out of Carmon.

Mike tried to doze, but his conversation with the doctor whirled through his mind, so feeling restless he went to the door. Brandon saw him and smiled.

'It's good to see you outside,' he said, coming over. 'So now that you've ventured out, will you join us to eat?'

Mike considered Brandon's hopeful smile.

'Later. For now, give me a gun.'

Brandon shook his head. 'That's not the way, Mike. Doctor Willis must have given you hope.'

'He did, and an idea, but for that I need a gun.' Mike waited, but Brandon said nothing, so he shrugged. 'Just give me one. I won't blow my brains out.'

'Then what do you want it for?' Brandon said, removing his gun from its holster and handing it over.

Mike glanced at Victor, who was looking elsewhere. Bearing in mind his previous antipathy towards him, Mike judged that he was making an especial effort to avoid looking at him.

'What sort of targets can Victor hit?'

Brandon smiled, his twinkling eyes showing that he understood what Mike was planning to do.

'I remember now that you taunted Victor about being able to outshoot him,' Brandon rummaged in his pocket and drew out an Indian Head cent, which he held up for Mike to inspect. Then he located a flat stone and placed the coin on the top, facing him. 'Victor can bore a hole clean through the Indian at twenty paces.'

For confirmation Brandon looked at Victor, who had turned to watch this discussion. He said nothing and folded his arms with a show of a surly lack of interest.

'Then turn it side on,' Mike said, raising his voice as much as he could to ensure Victor heard him, 'and I'll split it in two at thirty paces.'

Brandon rubbed his hands approvingly. Then he hurried away to turn the coin as instructed.

Mike didn't feel well enough to take thirty paces so he stayed where he was and sighted the coin. The gun felt unnaturally heavy and his hand shook, making him think he would probably miss, but holding a weapon and concentrating on something other then his own misery cheered him.

If he were ever to get revenge on the men who had tried to kill him, he needed to regain his strength and his old skills. And now was as good a time as any to begin that journey. So he imagined that the coin was Floyd Kelly's right eye, then made that image become Nyle Adams's left eye.

For a moment his hand steadied and he fired.

The kickback rattled his teeth and

delivered a jarring bolt of pain through his jaw that made him wonder whether it'd been a wise thing to do. But Brandon whistled with glee, then hurried over to the stone and rooted around on the ground.

A round of applause sounded and others joined him in the search. Victor stayed where he was and contented himself with glaring at Mike.

Presently, with a cry of triumph, Brandon found the coin and brought it over.

'You just winged it,' he said holding up the nicked coin for inspection. 'But after what you've been through that was well done.'

'And I'll get better.' Mike took the coin and pocketed it for luck, then handed Brandon the gun. 'And one day soon, I hope, I'll be able to repay the help you've given me by being good enough to be a part of your show.'

'Two sharpshooters is always better than one.' Brandon patted him on the back and grinned as the idea grew in his mind.

Mike looked at Victor, but he had already turned his back.

'How should I start?'

'You'll have to mend, of course, and practise a lot more, but the first thing you have to do is the easiest thing of all. You have to get used to your new name.' Brandon winked. 'From now on, Mike, you'll answer to Sharpshooter McClure.'

8

'Your aim's getting better,' Brandon said. 'Are you well enough to perform yet?'

Mike lowered the gun and rolled his shoulders, freeing the tension in his neck without moving his jaw.

'I'm ready,' he said. He glanced at the rest of the troupe who were gathered around the fire. Many were watching him, although the one who should have shown the most interest wasn't showing any. 'But before I stand before a paying audience I need to turn what I do into an act.'

Brandon nodded. They didn't need to discuss the subject of how Victor ignored the presence of another, better sharpshooter in their midst.

'I'll get him to talk to you,' Brandon said. He patted Mike's shoulder before he left him to complete his shooting practice.

The last two weeks had been a time of slow recovery.

Mike was haggard from weight loss, as he couldn't chew solid foods and could eat only broth and soups. Shooting still hurt, but every day his jaw was less sore than before and so he forced himself to fire more often.

He had been rewarded when most of his old accuracy had returned. But it came at the cost of incapacitating headaches that started in his neck and spread out until his head felt as if it were being trampled on by a herd of longhorns.

So he was a long way away from being fit enough to return to Harmony to take on Floyd and Nyle.

That acceptance of his frailty let him throw himself into his temporary new life as a sharpshooter. With the stitching having been taken out and the bandages having come off, for short periods he even managed to forget he'd been injured.

When he eventually holstered his gun

Victor came over and stood with his arms folded and his head cocked to one side as he appraised him.

'Brandon says you're ready to impress a paying audience,' he said. 'But you're no showman and you sure are an ugly critter. You'll make the women scream and we don't want that.'

Victor looked aside, his gaze picking out Eve with obvious meaning, before he looked back at Mike, licking his lips.

Mike tensed his sore jaw, accepting that his implication was right. Despite his having rescued Eve, and her initial interest in him, since the injury she had hardly spoken to him.

'I know, but I reckon we could both wear masks. That would hide my scars and add a sense of mystery about who we are.'

'Covering up your ugly face is a good idea, but being mysterious is only worth while if you're doing something people want to see.'

'I suggest we stand back to back and fire at identical targets.'

His original idea had been to fire at targets that were placed further away and got smaller, along the lines of the riders' competitive performances.

He was confident of winning such a competition, but as Victor would know that, this wasn't the right time to suggest it.

Victor considered the suggestion, his grinding jaw conveying that he knew this was an acceptable idea even if he couldn't bring himself to agree.

'That dull idea proves you've got no idea what an audience wants to see. I used to light a cigarette in Eve's mouth. I could do the same to you.' Victor smirked. 'Unless you don't trust my aim and you're worried I'll blow the rest of your face off.'

Mike forced a thin smile. 'I'm still recovering. I don't trust my aim enough yet.'

'Then you're certainly not trying it on my sister. She's too precious for me to let you do anything with her.' Victor shrugged. 'But if standing back to back is all you can do, I suppose we'll have to disappoint the audience with that.'

With that less than enthusiastic agreement to their act Victor returned to the fire and sat with Eve.

Mike was amused to see that she shuffled away from him, the disagreement that had happened between them clearly not having been sorted out yet.

'So you're going to perform, after all,' Brandon said when he came over to find out the result of their conversation.

'I'm looking forward to being Sharpshooter McClure.' Mike thought for a bit. 'And if you're open to new ideas, there's something else I could do.'

★   ★   ★

Mike's first performance went without a hitch.

They were in the small town of Dirtwood. Brandon had only stopped there to ask how far it was to the next town, but he'd had such an enthusiastic reception that he'd stayed.

141

They performed to twenty home-steaders who were too poor to provide anything other than food and hospital-ity, but starting off his new career before such a small and cheery audience was just what Mike needed.

As the audience supported every-thing enthusiastically, he couldn't be sure that he'd performed well, but he hit his targets and didn't argue with Victor, so he was content.

While Eve was singing, Brandon came over and slapped him on the back.

'A month ago you nearly died,' he said with a wide gesture at the audience, 'and now you're entertaining the public.'

'And I enjoyed it. So I'd like to do the second performance.'

Brandon smiled. 'Acting! You'll find that shooting is easy compared to the noble art of enchanting an audience with verbal trickery alone.'

'Does that mean I'll get some lines?'

'Not yet.' Brandon's gaze flickered

down to the mask Mike was wearing with an unspoken question that was also on Mike's mind.

'I need to do this or I'll never be able to start living again.' Mike removed the mask. 'On stage as an actor is the best way.'

Brandon agreed, so Mike headed back to the wagon. As he donned a suitably dark jacket, outside Eve finished her song, although tonight it would have less of a connection with the play than before.

With the audience containing many children and womenfolk, Lula and Belle danced in a less raucous manner than usual. Then Brandon stepped up on the stage to introduce the amended play. Mike's role was to be a minor one, but a significant one for him.

Brandon now played a ruthless rancher who was driving good-hearted homesteaders off their land. This received a sombre reaction from the audience, but when Mike peered out through the door, he reckoned they were involved in the story.

Eve played a woman who couldn't be driven away and who rallied the other homesteaders to defy Brandon as she awaited her husband's return. So Brandon hired a gunslinger to see her off. This was Mike's moment and he stepped up on to the stage to face the audience with his scarred cheeks held high.

A collective gasp echoed. Then from the audience someone barked out.

'They sure made him look real ugly!'

Laughter sounded, making Brandon look at Mike, but Mike winked. Perhaps later he might view that reaction differently, but they figured he'd been made to look like a gaunt and scarred gunslinger and he was prepared to settle for that.

The rest of the play was well received and the denouement gathered huge applause as Mike's revision let it stray close to his past. Mike tried to shoot up Eve, but then Victor arrived in the guise of a US marshal.

They faced each other in a show-down. After much posturing Victor drew first and killed him, his staged defeat making Victor smile for the first time in a while.

His death, followed by Eve's and Victor's embrace over his body drew forth cheers and cries for more, which continued as Eve sang her song to close the show.

Afterwards they broke with tradition and stayed in Dirtwood for the night, although, as the townsfolk milled around for a while, Mike stayed inside to avoid anyone seeing that he hadn't been in disguise.

His head was throbbing and the night's exertions had tired him more than they would have before his injury, but he reckoned he'd made a significant step forward in his recovery. So he studied the map on which Brandon plotted out their route.

Brandon avoided visiting anywhere twice, but he still planned to travel in a circle. That would bring them close to

Harmony in around three months.

'Perfect timing,' Mike said to himself, feeling his ridged jaw.

He folded the map with a determined swipe then turned to find he had company. Eve had come to see him.

'Your timing *was* good,' she said. 'You played your role well.'

Mike was sure she must have seen him studying the map, but as this was the first time they'd spoken in a while, he responded appropriately.

'I didn't have no lines,' he said. 'I only had to walk and die.'

'But it took guts to stand before those people while you're still mending.'

'I'll never mend fully, but they thought it was make-up, so perhaps I shouldn't be disappointed. I hope Brandon knows how to fashion a hooked nose and a hunched back and — '

'Stop that!' she snapped. 'Self-pity does you no favours. Your injury isn't that bad to look at.'

'It's bad enough to keep you away.'

She considered him, her grinding jaw and silence suggesting she was weighing up whether to provide the retort that had originally come to mind.

'I have stayed away,' she said at last, her voice low, 'but not because of how you look.'

'Victor?'

'Not him.'

Mike sighed. The evening had gone well and he didn't want to suffer a setback, but he felt he couldn't avoid the invitation.

'Then what is the reason?'

She paused before replying and when she spoke a suppressed emotion strained her voice.

'Everyone reckons I should be grateful to you for saving my life, but I know you didn't save me. Like back in Redemption City with those two rowdy men, I was only ever in danger because of you.'

Mike nodded then backed away to sit on a corner of the bed.

'How did you work that out?'

'It was obvious. I was kidnapped and a kidnapping needs someone to know the victim has been taken so that they can pay the price for their release. You were the one who had to pay the price, and you sure did that.'

'I did,' Mike said, feeling the tender scar tissue on his cheeks. 'I remember that every time I try to eat and every time anyone looks at me.'

'And I'd like to feel sorry for you, but I don't know why he tried to kill you. Everybody has forgotten how we found you, washed up beside the river near Harmony, half-drowned. There was a reason for you being in that river and I reckon it had something to do with the man who shot you.'

Mike winced. The first time he'd spoken with Brandon he'd vowed not to tell him about the events in Harmony, judging that such knowledge would invite retribution. So he certainly couldn't risk Eve's life.

'Please don't question me about that.'

148

'I don't have to. I can see the answer in your eyes. Something got you out of bed and forced you to practise shooting for all those hours despite the pain, and it wasn't to become Sharpshooter McClure.'

'For now I am Sharpshooter McClure, and that's all that should matter to everyone here.'

'But not me. I saw you looking at that map, wondering when we'll be close to Harmony. That is where that man came from, isn't it?'

Mike looked aloft. 'I said I didn't want to answer those sorts of questions. Why won't you listen to me?'

'Because . . . Because . . . ' She stamped a foot. 'Because I care for you and I thought you might one day take me away from all this.'

She sobbed with a single snort of sorrow then put a hand to her mouth as if she'd said too much.

'I know you argue with your brother, but I didn't know you weren't happy here.'

'There's plenty you don't know, you numbskull.' She backed away, her face reddening, perhaps in embarrassment. 'I shouldn't have opened my heart to you. You'll still go after him. And then you'll just get yourself killed.'

'I might not, and afterwards I could return.'

He surprised himself with his comment, as until now he hadn't thought about what he would do after he had returned to Harmony.

She stopped in the doorway.

'If you go, when you return I'll be gone. But if you stay with me, we could go somewhere together where you'll be safe and I can stop . . . ' She trailed off and gulped to stop herself sobbing again.

'I have to go. You must know that.'

She stayed looking at him, her eyes watering. Then without further comment she slipped outside into the darkness.

* ★ ★

150

Mike's first two months as a sharp-shooter in Brandon's show passed quietly.

He bided his time with regard to his desire for revenge and became as valuable a part of Brandon's entourage as everyone else was. When they put on a show he performed his routine with Victor, although they never talked about it, or anything else for that matter.

After her revelation, Eve avoided him, so their friendship didn't develop.

He didn't know whether that was because she was embarrassed at admitting she had feelings for him or because she was worried about his troubled past and his future aims.

She often argued with Victor, but he didn't know why and he was sure the siblings wouldn't welcome him interfering.

Either way, he kept an eye on them in case Victor's temper brimmed over and he hit her. This was something Mike resolved would be the last thing he did.

Although Brandon refused to give him lines to speak, he developed the play by adding in more details from the events at Harmony. This helped to keep the massacre fresh in his mind and to maintain his determination to take on Floyd and Nyle.

To that end, they slowly approached Harmony. The closest point would come in two weeks at Prudence, the town where he'd been a deputy sheriff, by which time his recovery would be complete.

His jaw no longer ached and he could talk clearly. He'd learnt to chew and to manage without the missing teeth. The move to normal food meant his weight and strength were returning to their previous levels.

Headaches still pained him if he moved his jaw too often, but they didn't come as often as before. He'd avoided the lopsided jaw Doctor Willis had feared and although the scar tissue was no longer inflamed it was too extensive to let him grow a covering beard.

Despite this, he no longer felt himself to be a repulsive sight and when he arrived on stage, instead of gasps of horror he received murmured comments that everyone could tell he was the evil gunslinger.

As for his life as a sharpshooter, it followed a predictable routine enlivened by occasional bouts of frenetic excitement.

Sometimes they left town in a hurry after Brandon argued with a saloon owner. Other times men chased them out of town or followed them, but at those times everyone rallied around to repel the raiders.

So when, after their latest show, they stopped five miles out of Bear Creek, Mike wasn't surprised when several riders approached their wagons.

As always, some showfolk carried on as if nothing were untoward while others drifted into the shadows to be in position to deal with any trouble that erupted.

This time they'd come in greater

numbers than was usual.

Eight riders pulled up beyond the semicircle of wagons and considered them. They muttered to each other.

Then one man, whom Mike recognized with surprise as the bartender from Redemption City, Kurt Rogers, gestured, directing half their number to peel away and circle around the wagons while he and the other three men headed closer.

Kurt's actions removed any doubt that he meant trouble. So, following the usual pattern, more people slipped away to seek the cover of the wagons leaving Brandon, Victor and Mike sitting by the fire.

Brandon glanced at Mike then nodded to the side, ordering him to take up his usual position, but Mike shook his head, resolving to take a leading role for the first time. When the riders drew to a halt, Brandon nodded again, then turned to Kurt.

'What are you doing so far from home?' he asked, in a pleasant tone.

'I heard you were heading east,' Kurt said, 'so I gathered together a welcoming committee in Bear Creek to stop you coming anywhere near Redemption City.'

Mike rose to his feet and made his way over to stand beside Brandon. He placed a casual hand on his hip beside his holster.

'If you saw the show in Bear Creek,' he said, 'you'll remember me. I played the gunslinger. I died, but I was playing a part. I was also one of the masked men, and I wasn't playing a part when I lit a flying match. The other sharpshooter is behind me waiting to match me shot for shot.'

Kurt glanced at his companions, who returned nervous looks that said the truculence that had driven their leader to ride hundreds of miles to meet them didn't burn in their blood. Accordingly they backed their horses away a pace, closely followed by Kurt.

'Remember this,' Kurt said, pointing at Brandon. 'Don't go no further east or you'll regret it.'

With that comment the riders turned and made a slow passage away from the wagons.

Mike watched them depart. He had just noticed that the other four riders hadn't joined them yet when, with a cry of bravado, those riders came galloping through the gaps between the wagons.

Two riders jumped down from their horses and ran into hiding beside a wagon. The other two unfurled whips, which they slashed from side to side, making the showfolk who had backed away to the wagons run to avoid the flicks of rawhide.

Mike noted that to date the show-folk's periodic defences of their property had been accomplished with minimal bloodshed and with some style, but these men were more determined than the others had been.

Amongst the chaos Mike caught Brandon's eye to ask him how they should proceed. The stern look Brandon gave to Mike's holster left him in no doubt that they might have to use deadly force to prevail.

Mike was still reluctant to wound these men, so he picked out the nearest whip-holder. As the man raised the whip to strike a cowering Dexter, he shot at the whip, slicing a slither from the handle.

A second shot severed it and sent the rawhide flying. By now the other riders had turned and were heading back to the wagons, but Mike put them from his mind and turned to the other whip-holder.

Victor reacted first. A shot to the man's forearm sent the whip flying from his grasp. As the man clutched his arm Sheridan threw a rope. It dropped down to tighten around the man's upper arms.

With the whips taken care of, the showfolk employed their usual efficient tactics.

Another rope took care of the other rider.

Three men surrounded one of the

157

men on foot and, with a few solid blows, pummelled him to the ground. The women combined to take on the other man. This confused him into not returning a single blow, which he soon regretted when Little Feather delivered a slap to the cheek that flattened him.

As each group held their attacked man down, Kurt's other riders galloped back towards them.

Mike watched them, waiting to see what form of attack they'd launch, but at the last moment they swung to the side and went around the backs of the wagons.

He caught glimpses of the horses as they passed between the wagons, and everyone who wasn't holding a raider down watched them, waiting for them to emerge at the other end. But when the horses appeared, they were rider-less.

A moment later the first man darted around the end wagon on foot, gun in hand. He blasted lead at the showfolk, scattering them into hiding.

While Victor took up a position side-on to the wagons Mike stayed where he was and hunkered down, judging his position to be one where he could see well.

Everyone had reached the relative safety of the wagons when a gun slipped around the other end of the wagon. However, the man didn't get to fire before Mike blasted the gun from his hand.

Then two men risked running out from the other end of the wagon with another man staying back to cover him. Neither man got far.

Mike shot the gun from the covering man's hand, then tried to do the same to the others. This time the urgency of the situation hurried him into an ill-aimed shot, and he slammed lead into one man's gun hand instead.

A screech rent the air and the man went down, clutching his bloodied hand, before he joined the other man in scurrying back into hiding.

'Nice shooting, Mike,' Victor called

out, his tone sarcastic. 'At least you've realized we're not getting out of this without bloodshed.'

Mike didn't respond and took the opportunity to reload. Then he roved his gun from side to side, taking in the ends of the wagon. But when he saw movement it came from an unexpected place.

In the shadows beneath the wagon Kurt was edging forward. Mike swung his gun towards him, but before he could fire Victor got him in his sights. A gunshot roared.

Kurt screeched, then rolled away to lie partly in the light. His gun fell from his slack fingers, his other hand clutched his bloodied chest.

'That's enough!' a raider shouted from the shadows. 'Don't shoot.'

Mike watched Kurt squirm, twitch, be still then looked at Victor, who was licking his lips eagerly while keeping his gun on the wagons as he waited for anyone else to come into view.

'You heard them, Victor,' Mike said.

'Let them give themselves up.'

'I don't trust them,' Victor snapped. 'The first one to show gets what Kurt got.'

Mike glared at the determined Victor then turned to face the wagons.

'You heard him. You're in big trouble if you don't surrender immediately. So throw down your guns and come out reaching for the sky.'

'We heard the other one,' someone shouted from the shadows. 'He'll kill us.'

'I promise you, if he shoots an armed man, I'll plant another bullet in that man.' Mike swung his gun to the side to pick out Victor. 'But if he shoots an unarmed man, it'll be the last thing he does.'

Victor glanced at Mike, to see that he had turned a gun on him. Anger reddened his face, making Mike think he'd ignore the raiders and face him down.

Before he could react, the raiders' willingness to fight died with the death of the man who had hired them. One by one they hurled their guns out. Then with their hands raised they emerged and joined the other captured men.

Mike holstered his gun without catching Victor's eye.

Then, with the situation under control, the showfolk followed their usual procedure after foiled raids, but this time with greater urgency and without good cheer. They ran off the horses, disarmed the men who were still armed, then delivered stern warnings not to return, before they ran everyone away.

The men left quietly, although the last man broke off from helping to carry Kurt's body away to fix Brandon with a surly eye.

'Kurt paid us,' he grunted, 'but we didn't need no encouragement after what you did. So remember this: you're not welcome in Redemption City and you'd better avoid Bear Creek too if you know what's good for you.'

Then he followed the other men.

Everyone waited until the men had receded into the darkness. Then a subdued cheer went up and some of the former good cheer returned.

Brandon issued orders for two men to patrol the compass points throughout the night while the rest tried to return to normalcy. Before Victor joined the first watch he came over to Mike.

'You turned a gun on me,' he said in a matter-of-fact manner that contained a hint he had been impressed.

'Sure did,' Mike said. 'I couldn't let you kill indiscriminately.'

'I saw that.' Victor leaned towards him. 'But just so you know: do that again and I'll kill you.'

With that warning made in a pleasant manner Victor turned his back on him and headed away from the wagons.

Mike watched him leave, then kicked at the dirt in irritation as Brandon joined him.

'I'm mighty pleased that we had you with us,' Brandon said.

'I'm pleased to be here too. Victor

could have turned that skirmish into a bloodbath.'

'I didn't mean that. Tonight, you became at last a complete part of our group.' Brandon shrugged. 'And maybe you could have defended us without killing any of them. But we'll never know anything for sure, other than that those men attacked us and Victor acted to save us.'

'I might be being too hard on him,' Mike said, conceding Brandon's point so as to end the arguments for the night. 'After all, it was Kurt's fault for riding all that way to attack us.'

Brandon rubbed his chin. 'Well, not that I can blame him, of course.'

Mike narrowed his eyes. 'What do you mean?'

For several seconds Brandon didn't reply. His brow furrowed. He looked around with a bemused expression on his face. Then he looked at Mike with his hands on his hips.

'If you get any better at this acting, I'll have to give you lines.' He watched

Mike frown. 'This is you acting, isn't it?'

'No. Why did Kurt and the rest of those men think they'd been wronged?' Mike cast his mind back. 'And for that matter, you're as friendly a group of people as I've ever met, and yet you attract one hell of a lot of aggrieved raiders and disgruntled townsfolk.'

'I know, and that's why we leave town as soon as we've performed.'

Mike raised his eyebrows. 'You mean you expect to be raided?'

'Of course we do.' Brandon chuckled, then slapped Mike on the back. 'You really don't know, do you? All this time you've spent with us and you've never realized how we make our money.'

'How?' Mike murmured.

'We steal,' Brandon said.

9

'All the raiders we've fended off were only trying to get back their stolen property?' Mike murmured aghast.

'Yes,' Brandon said with a shrug, his expression still bemused that Mike thought their actions were wrong. 'We run a show. Do you really think we make enough money to survive by passing around a pail? We have to take whatever we can.'

'But not by stealing, surely?'

Brandon spread his hands. 'We have no choice. When we ride into town, everybody tries to use us. We're just ensuring we get the cut we deserve by doing to them what they plan to do to us.'

'How?'

'When we perform outside a saloon we agree a cut of the additional income our presence will raise. The saloon owners never give us our full due so while everyone is distracted, usually by Belle and Lula's dancing, we make a sneak raid on the saloon. Someone usually finds out later and comes after us, but we run them off.'

'This is wrong, Brandon.'

Brandon shook his head. 'Why are you so shocked? You're not a lawman.'

'No,' Mike said. 'I'm not a lawman. A lawman would have worked out what you were doing a long time ago.'

★   ★   ★

Mike stepped up on to the stage in Prudence for what would be his final show.

Nobody knew it was to be his final show, and he'd not decided yet whether he'd ignore the information he'd learnt or act upon it. This was partly because he owed these people his life, and partly because he was embarrassed that he'd not realized what they were doing.

Either way he couldn't stay with

these people whom he had considered his friends, but whom he now knew were the kind of people he would have arrested in the former life he'd led in this very town.

He was pleased that nobody had recognized him; not that he had expected them to. He had been in Prudence for only a week and that had been some time ago when he'd not been scarred or a member of a travelling show.

He was about to perform his last scene in the frequently amended play in which Victor, in his guise as a US marshal, defeated Brandon's hired gun when he tried to massacre the home-steaders.

Accordingly Mike sneered and pos-tured before Victor to a chorus of boos from the gathered crowd.

They had taken over the road outside the saloon and Belle was taking the last opportunity to pass around a pail. Mike couldn't help but notice that Dexter and Sheridan were slipping in to the saloon at the back of the crowd, presumably on a mission to steal while everyone was distracted.

That sight removed the doubt from Mike's mind as to what his next actions must be. While he milked the crowd with his arrogant swaggering he glanced down the road. The law office was at the end of the road and a light was on. He nodded to himself then turned to face Victor.

The crowd quietened as the two actors faced each other in a showdown, as they had done numerous times before.

Victor smirked, presumably remembering the incident outside Bear Creek, while Mike spat to the side, sneered, then moved for his gun, his hand creeping towards his holster in an obvious gesture that nobody could miss.

'He's going for his gun!' a child shouted in the crowd, obviously taken up in the excitement, before he was promptly hushed.

Then, before the tense moment was lost, Mike swung his hand to his holster. He drew, but with a quicker motion Victor drew, crouched and fired.

Mike staggered a pace forward, clutching his chest. Brandon's instructions were that he should remain silent while he keeled over, but on a whim he staggered another pace to stand toe to toe with Victor.

He looked him in the eye. Then he rocked a short-armed jab into his stomach that bent him double, followed by a round-armed punch to his chin that lifted his feet off the stage before he thudded to the ground on his back.

'Don't ever hurt her,' he said, peering over the side of the stage, 'or I'll come back and haunt you.'

Then he glanced at Brandon, who had been busy surrendering now that his plans had failed, and fell to the stage. From there he listened to the last scene play itself out, along with some improvisation from Brandon and Eve to cover the fact that Victor was lying beside the stage groaning.

While Eve sang her last song Brandon and Mike slipped off the stage. Brandon cast him an odd glance that appeared to show he knew why he'd hit Victor, but Mike didn't want to debate the issue. His mind was made up.

He waited until Eve had finished so that the bustle of the contented crowd would cover him. Then he slipped away quietly and headed down the road to the law office.

He walked purposefully, neither relishing nor dreading what was to come. He just had to do it before he left the show to embark on the other duty he couldn't avoid, and doing it in the town where he'd been deputized was an appropriate place to sever the ties he'd made.

At the door he stopped, rolled his shoulders, and took a deep breath. From inside he heard Sheriff Simmons talking. Hearing his voice for the first time in a while relaxed him.

He moved to open the door, but a hand slapped down on his shoulder. He swirled round, expecting to see that Brandon had followed him, but found that Eve had come.

'Don't,' she said.

'How do you know what I'm planning to do?' he asked.

'Because you just knocked Victor off the stage. It's clear you're going to do something stupid and then leave us.' She placed a hand on his arm. 'But if I mean anything to you, please don't report us to Sheriff Simmons.'

'I have to. Somebody has to know what you're doing.' He remembered a conversation they'd had two months ago. 'And you know that. That's why you hoped I'd take you away from this show. You don't like the stealing either.'

'I don't, but we helped you. You can't repay our kindness by acting like a self-righteous fool or a law . . . ' She narrowed her eyes then intoned her final words while nodding with understanding. 'Or like a lawman.'

'You're right.' Mike smiled. 'I am a lawman.'

He'd thought he'd never say those words again, but the moment he did, the injury that had come to control his life no longer felt important.

'So that explains it.' She stood to the side. 'So go on. Enforce the law. Go in there and tell the sheriff what we've done, and lose all the good friends, and perhaps more that you've found here.'

Her voice caught, making Mike wish that he'd sought her out to clarify what they meant to each other. But before he could voice his thoughts about her the office door opened and Sheriff Simmons emerged.

'You want me?' Simmons asked, turning to face him.

Mike gulped, the sight of his old mentor making him forget his planned statement. Then he saw the lawman's blank expression. He didn't recognize him, and that was fine with Mike. He didn't want to be recognized when he had unfinished business in Harmony.

To cover his confusion he looked at Eve. She glared at him, her eyes pleading. Finding no comfort there he turned back to the lawman.

'I do,' he said. 'I want to report a crime at Brandon Webb's show.'

Simmons sighed then gestured for the people in the office to follow him out.

'Then you'll have to join the queue.'

With that cryptic comment Sheriff Simmons headed down the road towards the show. Barney Root, the saloon's bartender, followed him closely followed by a crying woman who was being comforted by a new deputy.

Mike cast a bemused glance at Eve, but he received a stern glare that said he had already gone too far. Mike offered her an apologetic smile, then set off with the train of people.

Before they reached the wagons Brandon saw them coming, but he put on a good show of being busy and not noticing them until the sheriff was standing before him. Brandon flinched, then let his gaze rise slowly to take in the sheriff. A smile appeared.

'I'm afraid the show's over, Sheriff,' he said in a light tone, 'but don't you worry. I'm sure we — '

'Quit the fancy talk,' Simmons barked. 'Barney here has accused you of thieving.'

Brandon gave a significant glance to the nearest showfolk, a look that silently asked everyone to be prepared for trouble. Then he faced Barney.

'While everyone was watching the play,' Barney said, 'one of your people sneaked into my saloon and stole a hundred dollars.'

Brandon sighed and spread his hands in a gesture of resignation.

'Sadly, that's the burden we travelling performers must bear. Everywhere we go we are strangers and strangers are blamed whenever something goes astray.' He waggled a finger at Barney and lowered his voice. 'But unless you have proof, keep your accusations to yourself.'

'Enough!' Simmons snapped as Barney started to argue. Then he gestured to the woman, who had been snuffling to herself, to come forward and speak.

'While I was giving one of your performers money,' she said, fingering her neck as she faced Brandon, 'I lost my treasured gold locket. I felt a tug at the neck, but didn't realize until later that she must have torn it away.'

Brandon dismissed the matter with a snort that said he wouldn't dignify this accusation with a response, leaving the sheriff to ask the obvious question.

'Who did it?'

The woman swung round and pointed at Eve.

'We do not steal gold lockets,' Brandon snapped while Eve threw a hand to her mouth, 'from ladies such as yourself.'

His aggrieved response sounded convincing, but then again Mike had seen him act on stage and knew he was good at it.

For several seconds silence reigned as

Victor glared at Eve, his face red with anger.

Mike assumed that his expression meant he was preparing to fight his way out of the bad situation, then he saw the shamefaced glance Eve shot at her brother.

In a moment Mike understood what had caused the siblings' frequent arguments, and perhaps why Eve had really wanted to leave the show.

Brandon might have organized expeditions to steal from the saloons, but these two stole from the spectators too. Whether Brandon and the others knew about this he couldn't tell, but either way it was clear what his next actions must be.

He folded his arms and backed away a pace, planning to play no part in the justice Sheriff Simmons would hand out. And he accepted that his time with Brandon's show was destined to end in the sourest way possible.

'There's only one way to sort this out,' Simmons said. 'You'll all come to the law office while my deputy searches your wagons.'

'No!' Victor shouted, raising a hand and gathering everybody's attention. 'There's no need to search us. I know who really did it.'

'Who?'

Victor looked around the showfolk, many of whom stared at him in bemusement. Victor's perusal ended with him looking at Mike.

'As Brandon said, Barney blamed us only because we're strangers. But that works for us too. One man joined us recently and we've only faced trouble since he arrived.' Victor pointed at Mike and raised his voice. 'Search him and you'll find out the truth.'

Brandon started to complain, but Simmons demanded he be quiet. Then, with the weary air of a man who was tired of them all and knew he was facing a long night of accusation and counter-accusation, he came over to Mike.

'Open your jacket,' he said.

Mike now wished that he'd told the sheriff who he was earlier, but he probably wouldn't believe his tale now. So he did as ordered.

As Simmons rooted through his pockets Mike looked over the sheriff's shoulder at Victor while wondering what his real motives were.

Then Simmons tensed. An eyebrow raised. Slowly he drew his hand out of Mike's side pocket and dangling from his fingers was a gold locket.

'I've never seen that before,' Mike murmured as the aggrieved woman shrieked with joy.

'If I had a dime for every time I've heard that,' Simmons said, shaking his head.

'You'd be able to retire,' Mike said, completing a sentiment he'd heard several times in his week as Simmons's deputy.

The sheriff narrowed his eyes as Mike's comment set off a train of thought. He considered Mike's scarred cheeks, then looked him in the eye. The unspoken question hovered on his lips, but he shook his head, dismissing the thought, and turned to the woman to carry out the formalities of confirming that the locket was the stolen one.

When the contented woman wandered off with her property, he gestured for his deputy to begin the arrests.

'Surely,' Brandon said, backing away before the advancing deputy, 'we can sort this out without further unpleasantness.'

'I'm open to suggestions,' Simmons said. 'I don't want you bunch of worthless varmints cluttering up my jailhouse if I can avoid it.'

Brandon raised a hand then uttered a forlorn sigh.

Two minutes later the delighted Barney headed back to his saloon with the pail of money tucked under an arm. His smirk suggested the pail contained more than the one hundred dollars he claimed to have lost.

'And now that you've made us into paupers, can we leave?' Brandon said, frowning at the sheriff.

'I'm still minded to make an example of you.' Simmons cast Brandon a sneering look. 'But on the other hand I'd welcome it more if you never stepped foot in Prudence again.'

'We won't, but this matter won't end here.' Brandon lowered his voice to a serious tone. 'We did not steal that locket and whether you believe me or not, rest assured, Sheriff, we sort out our problems ourselves. Before this night is through, one of our group will feel our wrath.'

★   ★   ★

The informal court was in session.

The wagons had been drawn up into a circle five miles out of Prudence. Then everyone had sat around the edges with Brandon taking up a leading position standing beside his wagon.

Since Sheriff Simmons had run them out of town Mike had had no choice but to stay with them. But the harsh

181

glares everyone had shot at him had left him in no doubt that they wouldn't accept his leaving before they got to the truth.

'Before tonight we all trusted each other,' Brandon said, his tone containing none of his usual jocular manner. 'But now that trust has been betrayed and we cannot go on until we know the truth.'

Grunts of support came from around the circle of watchers. Mike didn't join in and he noticed that neither did Eve and Victor.

'We steal from those who would steal from us,' Brandon continued, 'but we do not target our customers. We cherish them. And yet tonight someone stole a gold locket. That is unacceptable.'

Hands slapped to the ground registering support and Mike was pleased to see the accusing glances that were cast around weren't all directed at him. He also found his opinion of the showfolk changing again.

He didn't approve of their methods,

but he saw that their logic made sense. They clearly did only steal out of necessity from those who sought to make undeserved profit out of them.

As Brandon said nothing else, he thought that this was the right time for him to speak. He stood up, gathering everyone's attention.

'I did not steal that locket,' he said. 'The first time I saw it was when Sheriff Simmons drew it out of my pocket.'

He received a quiet response, only a few people murmuring in a non-committal manner.

'Can you prove that?' Brandon asked.

'No. I can only say that I don't approve of you stealing and I was planning to leave tonight. I would not have stolen before going.'

'I didn't know you were leaving, but I do know you were shocked to discover we stole.' Brandon rocked his head from side to side. 'Unless anyone has any information to the contrary, I believe you.'

Mike breathed a sigh of relief. He

was pleased to note that several people looked at Victor a moment before Victor leapt to his feet.

'I know the full story,' he shouted. 'He was going to the sheriff to betray us. So Eve tried to stop him.'

Despite Victor having ignored Brandon's request for information about the locket, the mention of a new name made everyone look at Eve.

She coughed, got to her feet, then looked around the circle, finishing with her gaze on Mike.

'He wasn't going to betray us,' she said with a shaking voice. 'He went to the law office because we're close to the place where he was nearly killed. He wanted to ask the sheriff if he knew about the man who shot him.'

Mike avoided reacting to her surprising support, not knowing for sure why she'd lied and defied her brother. Whatever the reason was, it brought to a head the arguments that had been simmering between her and Victor.

Victor stormed towards her, his face

reddening, his hand raised ready to hit her. She ducked away from the blow, but it never arrived. Mike had taken two long paces to reach them. He caught Victor's wrist on the backward swipe.

Victor strained, but when he found that Mike's grip was firm, he swirled round to face him.

'I haven't forgotten you hit me earlier,' Victor said, 'so get your thieving hand off me or I'll break your jaw again.'

'As I told you earlier,' Mike said, 'you will not hit your sister.'

'This is a family matter. It has nothing to do with you.'

'It has everything to do with me when you've been using this show as a cover to steal in every town we've visited and when you tried to cover that up by framing me.'

Victor smirked, his expression seeming pleased with this revelation.

'An accusation like that without proof can have only one answer.'

'And we know what that is,' Eve shouted. 'We need to see the proof and I can — '

'Be quiet!' Victor snapped. 'Mike knows what I meant and he's been hoping for a chance to find out ever since he joined the show. Now is the time to prove which of us is the sharpshooter showman and which one can do it for real.'

'If you insist,' Mike said. 'I know you've only been a sharpshooter, but you don't know what I did before you found me washed up by the river.'

He rubbed his scarred jaw with an obvious gesture to worry Victor into thinking about his past life. In response Victor narrowed his eyes, but gave no other reaction to the taunt.

Mike released his grip and backed away, keeping Victor in his view, while Victor also paced into clear space. Eve screeched at them to stop but the other women came over to comfort her and urge her to quieten.

Mike expected that Brandon would

speak up and stop this showdown while he still could, but aside from directing everyone to get out of the firing line, he said nothing.

In the centre of circle of wagons they stopped and faced each other, the fire to their side, the showfolk pressed against the wagons, watching silently.

'Your boast doesn't impress me,' Victor said. 'I've seen you shoot. You're accurate, but you're not a fast draw. You haven't the experience to take me on. Scurry away into hiding while you still can.'

Mike had to admit he didn't need this battle, but Victor had said the one thing that ensured he couldn't avoid it.

Marshal Jesse Cole had once said he didn't have the experience to deal with fraught situations, and he had been proved right when the homesteaders had been massacred. But to be sure that he could take on Floyd and Nyle, he needed to prove himself here.

For the last few months he hadn't widened his experience beyond acting as a gunslinger, but maybe acting was all he needed to have done. So he settled his stance, rolled his shoulders, and spat to the side in the same arrogant way that he used every time they performed their play just before Victor drew first and killed him.

The sight made Victor snort out a burst of laughter and look around the gathered people to see if they'd noticed the similarity.

That was the distraction Mike had wanted.

He threw his hand to his holster. The gun came to hand in a moment. He drew, crouching forward with the action. As Victor drew his own gun, without taking care over his aim Mike blasted a single shot through Victor's chest.

Victor staggered backwards, his own ill-directed shot wasting itself in the dirt. He met Mike's gaze for a moment with a look that registered an emotion, perhaps surprise. Then he keeled over.

Mimicking the action Victor made

after every performance Mike twirled his gun back in his holster, then stood with his arms folded watching Eve hurry over to her brother's still body.

For the first time he had shot to kill. Worse, he had shot Victor while he'd been distracted and he wouldn't have done that before his recent experiences, but he was relieved that his success bought him no pleasure.

'You could have just wounded him,' Eve screeched, leaning over Victor's body.

Mike shrugged. 'I could have tried, but I know I'm lucky to be alive and that luck might not have held again. Mike McClure didn't know that but Sharpshooter McClure sure does.'

She looked at him, his cryptic comment making her furrow her brow, as Brandon came over to join him.

'This probably means we'll never prove what really happened,' Brandon said, 'but I need a sharpshooter, so I still hope you'll stay with us. And I hope you've seen that we're not as bad as you feared we were.'

Mike considered, then provided a firm nod.

'I accept you're not bad people and maybe if I didn't have other things to do I'd stay. But ever since you found me beside that river you've always known I'd have to leave one day.' Mike fingered his ruined cheeks.

Brandon considered Mike's scars, then nodded.

'I understand, but remember, we showfolk stick together. No matter what your problem is with whoever did that to you, it's our problem too.'

Mike smiled. 'Obliged, but this is something I have to do on — '

'Brandon!' Dexter shouted from the wagons. 'You need to see this.'

Everyone turned to see that Dexter and Sheridan had been investigating Eve and Victor's wagon. Both men were holding up handfuls of trinkets.

The revelations of the next few hours surprised everyone.

An investigation of the wagon revealed

an array of jewellery, coins and other valuables. Once they were laid out in the centre of the circle, Brandon reconvened the informal trial.

Eve denied nothing. In a monotone and honest sounding voice she told them the story of how she and Victor had operated.

For the last two years they had stolen secretly. If they needed to pickpocket, she had taken the valuables. For the trickier operations she would distract the victim while Victor stole.

The endeavour had started as a temporary activity to repay a debt Victor had incurred, but when that had been dealt with Victor had wanted more, to avoid ever getting into debt again.

He had promised the spree would end when he had enough. But he never had enough and Eve had increasingly begun to fear for her life if she were to cross a man who could shoot like Victor did.

When she completed her story

everyone waited for Brandon's pronouncement on her fate.

'Innocent people have suffered,' he said. 'But I believe that Victor was to blame. I say you can stay, but we accept the group's decision.'

As Eve murmured that she was sorry, Brandon looked at Dexter, the nearest person in the circle of the informal jury. Without hesitation Dexter gave an answer with the same sentiment.

When Sheridan and Big Man had supported the view that she had done wrong, but that if she stopped her activities, she could stay, Eve breathed more easily then began to cry.

For the next ten minutes the others gave the same verdict. Mike was the last to speak.

'I had planned to leave because I thought you were doing wrong,' he said. 'But perhaps there is a way to make this all right. You never return to the places you've visited before for fear of what the saloon owners you stole from will do, but maybe you should. And if you get challenged about what Eve and Victor did, you can return the property they stole.'

This idea got a supportive murmuring.

'We'll do that,' Brandon said, 'but you just said that you *had* planned to leave. Have you changed your mind?'

Mike took a deep breath. 'I have. Everywhere you've gone you've bought joy to many and misery to a few. And not always to the right people. So I reckon it's time for you to make amends and bring misery to the people who really deserve it.'

Mike rubbed his scarred cheeks with an obvious gesture that divulged his real motive, making Brandon smile.

'Do you know of people who are even more sneaky than Barney Root?'

'I sure do,' Mike said.

'And where are these people?'

Mike smiled, then pointed north. 'They are to be found near to a small town that you once visited. It's called Harmony.'

193

10

'So this is where it happened?' Brandon said.

'It did,' Mike said, looking around the burnt-out stable. 'I thought you needed to see it first so you'd know why we have to do this.'

He had brought Brandon into the shell of the stable in Harmony, but there was nothing to see other than the charred walls. The rest of the town had been burnt to the ground too, as had other distant buildings. They had yet to see any people, and all they had heard was the distant lowing of cattle.

'I can barely recognize this place.'

'That's because it's not the place you visited. That was a town with people and hope, but Harmony is no longer a community. It's just a valley within Nyle Adams's territory.'

'Except twelve innocent men died here.'

Mike nodded. 'Twelve men with families that you performed to and who enjoyed your show.'

Mike hoped that Brandon wouldn't ask how he knew that, but thankfully Brandon merely nodded.

'They sure did.' Brandon sighed. 'It was probably the last enjoyable thing they did before they were executed.'

Mike glanced around the charred wooden walls, remembering the carnage he'd witnessed here. He ended his perusal by looking at the spot where Marshal Jesse Cole had died. Then he turned back to Brandon.

'We can't bring them back, but the men responsible are over there.'

Mike pointed. Brandon swung round to look towards the horizon and Nyle Adams's distant ranch house.

'Then let's do it,' he said.

★　★　★

'How far is it to Harmony?' Brandon asked.

Two of Nyle Adams's ranch hands peeled away from the ranch gate to consider the line of wagons.

'Back along the way you came,' one man said, pointing. 'You must have ridden past it.'

'But then again,' the other man said, 'there's not much in the way of a town there no more. You'll have more luck with whatever you're looking for in Prudence or Redemption City.'

'That's a pity,' Brandon said, pouting. 'We'd planned to stop in Harmony as we'd enjoyed our previous stay there so much.'

The men glanced at each other.

'Who are you?'

'I am the legendary Brandon Webb, the owner of the greatest show in all the world.'

'Greatest show, eh?' The man glanced along the length of wagons. 'It don't look great to me.'

Brandon raised a finger. 'But that's only because you haven't seen the delights I have on offer.'

'Oh yeah?' The two ranch hands exchanged bored glances.

'We have the greatest sharpshooter in the land, the finest rope handlers, the greatest riders, the most fearsome war-chanting Cheyenne chief along with the most moving and exciting play ever performed.'

'That don't sound exciting.'

'I reckon,' the other man said, 'you should move on and bore somebody else with that.'

The two man chortled at their comments but, with a wink at Mike, Brandon maintained his smile.

'And there was one other delight I forgot to mention. Can you remember what it was, Sharpshooter McClure?'

Mike leaned back and put his hands behind his head, his exaggerated posture covering up his banging on the wooden wall behind him.

'Do you mean . . . ?'

'I surely do,' Brandon said, then put a hand to his ear.

Their actions made the ranch hands

glance at each other in bemusement. They turned to glare at Brandon.

'We don't care.'

'Yeah, just move on and . . . ' The man trailed off as his eyes alighted on the two women emerging from around the back of the wagon.

Belle and Lula were wearing the short skirts that had attracted so much attention in Redemption City. Both women sashayed down the length of the wagon then stood before each man, where they looked them up and down with frank appraising gazes.

What they saw made them nod approvingly. Then they looped arms around the men's shoulders while cooing and giggling.

'Ah, yes,' Brandon said, 'I remember now. We also have the dancing girls.'

'You surely do,' one man said, wiping the sudden outbreak of sweat from his brow as Lula ran a finger along his bristled jaw.

'And so,' Brandon said, 'if we can't present our show in Harmony, do you men know of anywhere else where these charming young ladies could perform?'

★　★　★

'I've seen this show before,' Floyd Kelly grumbled as Brandon moved towards the stage, 'and I didn't enjoy it then.'

'Be quiet,' Nyle Adams said. 'I'm looking forward to seeing it.'

He gestured for Brandon to get on and start the show, to which Brandon responded with a short bow.

'Then you'd better hope it has a better ending than the last time.' Floyd gave Nyle a significant glance that made him frown. 'They performed in Harmony a few months ago, and why anybody would return here after that, I don't know.'

'Ah,' Nyle murmured, then cast a confused glance at Brandon.

Before Nyle and Floyd could ask any worrying questions, Brandon hurried on to the stage, from where he looked along the line of the gathered audience.

In keeping with his normal policy he was starting the show at sundown. This had allowed everyone whom Nyle employed to gather at the front of his ranch house.

There were about thirty men in total, most appearing to be nothing more than ranch hands. These men were either leaning against or sitting on fences to watch the show, nudging and chatting to each other in eager excitement.

Brandon had already pinpointed who amongst them were Nyle's new hired guns. These men were congregated around Nyle, although until Floyd had cast doubts on their motives for being here, even these men had been in good spirits.

Brandon tried to rekindle those good spirits with a cheerful smile while he delivered his usual over-the-top boasts about the show to come. After which, with a grand gesture, he declared the show open.

As usual Logan and Clifford started

off by displaying their riding skills.

They rode off towards the ranch gates where they stopped and waited for Eve to remove the cover from the two stakes they'd erected. Then they galloped in and removed the revealed hats, which they twirled on to their heads, but if they'd expected applause, or even acknowledgement, they would have been disappointed.

The only person engaging the audience's interest was Eve.

Throughout the remainder of their act she continued to get catcalls and encouragement, even though she was only setting out the objects they had to collect. She responded with her usual good grace. When the riders finished their performance nobody even noticed they'd stopped riding. Quietly the two men slunk off to the side.

As Dexter and Sheridan started their lassoing demonstration to a chorus of complaints because Eve had slipped off behind a wagon, Brandon climbed into the wagon to join Mike, who was watching proceedings through a crack in the door.

'It's like you said,' Brandon said. 'They're not interested in anything we do.'

'In which case,' Mike said, smiling, 'everything is going according to plan.'

Brandon returned the smile, then joined Mike in watching how the lassoers fared. As it turned out, this act was received with even less enthusiasm than the riding had been. Without Eve to watch, the ranch hands had nothing to look at but the twirling ropes, and men who saw longhorns getting roped every day didn't view this as entertainment.

The ribald and initially good-natured grumbling gradually turned to outright abuse. Floyd was the ringleader of most of it.

Over the thirty yards that separated them Mike glared at him, imagining how the gunslinger would react when the man he thought dead appeared. Standing beside him was Nyle, who was also shifting uneasily.

'We want the dancing girls!' Floyd hollered, his voice cutting through the rising hubbub and making everyone laugh with a moment of shared disgust at the show.

Brandon slipped out of the door. He caught Dexter's eye and gave a brief nod. So he and Sheridan finished off their performance with one last high twirl before they gathered up their ropes. Then they followed Logan and Clifford in slinking off to the side and out of view.

Nobody watched them leave as everyone craned their necks in the hope that the only part of the show that interested them would be next. But Brandon again disappointed them. For this version of the show Mike wouldn't be sharpshooting, so Big Man and Little Feather came on next.

The presence of a woman in a short skirt gathered some interest and she got plenty of support when she enlivened her usual performance by wriggling and squealing while trying to escape Big Man's clutches. Big Man caught her eventually then tied her to the stake.

Then, encouraged by the better reaction they were getting, he lengthened his act with more posturing and by throwing the knives with more vigour than usual. As there was only one stake the knives flew past her and stuck into an unoccupied fence forty feet away.

This less spectacular display of his precision throwing didn't appear to disappoint anyone too much, as Little Feather was wailing and squirming in a way that kept everyone interested. And when the tomahawk appeared to sever her bonds the pair even got some applause.

They bowed to the audience, then hurried off to collect the knives. Everyone turned to watch Little Feather scurry off, but then all eyes turned to the front as Brandon introduced the only part of the show that really interested them.

Belle and Lula arrived.

Depending on the audience the women had a variety of acts they could perform. This time they went for the unsubtle performance.

Without music they jigged along the length of workers. They kicked up their legs, raised their skirts, and bent over repeatedly. All the time, they ensured they made eye contact with each man in turn.

Through the crack in the door Mike noticed that even Floyd was whistling and urging them on as he watched their every move, as did Nyle. Even the hired guns watched the women, showing that they hadn't been hired for their diligence or they would have noticed that after ending their performance Big Man and Little Feather hadn't returned to the wagons. And neither had any of the other performers.

Brandon watched the proceedings carefully, judging at which point he should step in and stop this part of the show. A convenient moment arrived when two boisterous men surged towards the women. The women saw them coming and backed away to avoid being gathered up in their outstretched arms.

Lula and Belle having stopped their dancing routine, calls for the men to get back so that they could continue tore out, followed by the men responding with surly comments and shaken fists. Not surprisingly a fight broke out, which only ended when the hired guns separated the rabble.

In the wagon Mike winced, realizing that if they'd known this would happen it would have been the perfect moment to act. Floyd and Nyle were both standing alone and making easy targets, but the moment passed as soon as it'd come.

The fighting men were dispatched to positions away from each other and Nyle barked out a demand for the show to carry on. Brandon used the moment to step up on to the stage.

'I reckon,' he called out, 'this is an appropriate moment to move on to the next act.'

'Who cares about the next act?' Floyd hollered. 'We're only here to see them.'

'And they will return when everyone has calmed down.'

'Then make sure it's a quick act.' Floyd thought for a moment, then pointed a firm finger at Brandon. 'And it'd better be more entertaining than that singer or the sharpshooter.'

Brandon smiled. 'And it is. I have great pleasure in presenting for your delight a short play.'

This revelation stunned Floyd into silence and while he exchanged an exasperated glance with Nyle, Brandon started his opening oration.

The play went down as well as any play being presented to a group of bored and surly ranch hands could go. The festering grumbling grew in volume even before anyone saw what the play was about. But then the story unfolded and, not surprisingly, this made Nyle call for quiet.

To a suddenly rapt audience Eve

delivered her lines in which she stated her hope that her husband, a US marshal, would return home to help her keep their property. Then Brandon went on to explain his plan to kill Eve and the other homesteaders who didn't leave what he saw as being his land.

'What kind of play is this?' Nyle shouted out.

'They were in Harmony,' Floyd grunted. 'They're mocking us.'

The ranch hands looked at Nyle and Floyd to gauge their reactions, while the hired guns edged towards the stage, anticipating their orders. Seeing that Nyle had become irked even sooner than expected, Brandon moved the play on apace.

'And so,' he declared, still hunched over in his conspiratorial manner, 'I reckon I'll hire me the finest gunslinger a man can buy to kill that meddling woman.'

This was Mike's cue. He opened the door of the wagon and stepped down. He was wearing his mask, but he still kept his head down as he paced on to the stage to join Brandon and Eve.

Brandon had still not allocated him lines, but he didn't need them to let the audience know his intentions. He placed his feet wide apart, then slowly looked up to consider the gathered ranch hands. Then he looked along them until he was staring directly at Nyle and Floyd.

Nyle was gesturing at the hired guns, giving them orders that presumably involved running the showfolk off his land, but Floyd wasn't listening to the orders. He was looking at Mike.

Mike centred his gaze on Floyd. He saw his narrowed eyes, his furrowed brow, the doubt in his mind as to what he was seeing.

Mike removed that doubt.

He reached up to the bow behind his ear that kept his mask in place and drew it open. Then he opened his hand and let the mask flutter to the stage.

Defiantly he thrust his chin high, letting Floyd see the scars of a man who had been shot from close range and who had survived.

Shock registered briefly in Floyd's eyes before he got himself under control.

'You,' he murmured.

11

With frantic arm movements Nyle
Adams urged his hired guns to run
Brandon off his land before he could
continue with any more of his play that
mocked his activities, but Mike ignored
him. He had eyes only for Floyd.

For long moments they looked at
each other. Neither man moved as
between them men scurried to carry
out Nyle's orders.

Then Mike saw a slight narrowing in
Floyd's eyes. He jerked his hand to his
gun. The weapon came to hand as, in a
blur of motion, Floyd reached for his
own gun. But by the time he'd drawn,
Mike had fired.

He didn't waste time on aiming carefully. He just shot at Floyd's body. He
was rewarded when his slug slammed
high into Floyd's chest sending him staggering backwards for a pace.

Floyd's return shot almost found its target when Mike felt the bullet catch his arm and fray cotton before it kicked splinters from the wagon behind him.

Floyd righted himself, his hand clutching the wound. Then he glared at him over twenty yards of ground, his gun rising slowly with a determination that said he would fire and hit him this time no matter what Mike did. But he didn't get to shoot. Mike planted a bullet in his forehead and sent him tumbling to the ground.

Then he turned his attention to his next target, but in the brief seconds he'd spent dispatching Floyd several of the ranch hands had come between him and Nyle as they rushed the stage, brandishing guns.

Mike dropped to one knee and picked off the nearest two men. Then the sheer volume of men charging the stage forced him to back away to the cover of the wagons, firing all the way. He'd lost sight of Brandon and Eve, but he hoped they'd found somewhere to go to ground.

From around the side of the blue-painted wagon he again tried to see where Nyle had gone, but he couldn't see him. Luckily he could see the showfolk who had sidled into hiding after their earlier performances and who were now ready to make their presence known.

Logan and Clifford came galloping in from the ranch gates, firing to the right and left, making the men before them scatter. Their horses bounded over any men who didn't move fast enough and Mike saw several men tumble to the ground as the horses barged into them.

At the same time Dexter and Sheridan crept over the roof of the ranch house, their arms and shoulders heavy with ropes which they laid out between them. Then they began to bloodlessly subdue Nyle's men by letting fly with the ropes. With unerring accuracy each landed on its target and drew tight around a chest.

Big Man showed no such inclination merely to incapacitate the ranch hands and from the safety of their position behind the fence Little Feather fed him one knife at a time. He took aim and let fly. Every knife buried itself in a target.

These assaults sent the men scattering in panic, everybody being unsure of the direction from which the next lethal attack would come. As the men thinned out Mike caught his first glimpse of Nyle since he'd killed Floyd. He was with five other men who all had the steely-eyed look of his hired guns. They were retreating to the ranch house.

Worse, they were dragging Eve and Brandon with them.

Mike loosed off a shot in anger as they slipped in through the door. Then he took stock of the situation.

He judged that the showfolk could deal with the remaining ranch hands, who were showing no sign of being able to stomach a fight. He didn't expect that the men Nyle had taken with him would view the situation in the same way.

While people were still milling around he made his way over to the ranch house, aiming to reach the corner of the building where only a few months ago he'd stopped while seeking to escape from Nyle's clutches.

He reached the spot without anyone firing at him. After checking that nobody was paying him undue attention, he dropped to his knees and worked his way along the porch beneath the windows to reach the door. He stood, keeping his back pressed to the wall and listened.

Inside people were talking. He heard Nyle's voice along with Brandon's and although he couldn't hear the words, Nyle's raised tone suggested he was questioning Brandon, presumably about why he'd launched this attack.

Mike reckoned that even with Brandon's knack of talking people round to his way of thinking, no answer would satisfy Nyle. So he prepared himself to kick open the door and barge in, but then he heard someone murmur his name from behind.

He turned at the hip with his gun held at the ready while crouching to confuse his assailant, but found that nobody was confronting him. The remaining ranch hands were being chased towards the ranch gates by Logan and Clifford. Big Man and Little Feather were collecting their knives from the sprawling bodies of their targets. Nobody else was showing any sign of putting up a fight.

'Mike, up here,' the voice said again. This time Mike looked up to the edge of the roof to see the upside-down face of Dexter looking at him and smiling. 'Count to ten, then burst in.'

'What you planning?'

'No time to explain,' Dexter said, showing him a length of rope. Then he glanced to the side and nodded, presumably to Sheridan, before jerking back out of view.

'But what . . . ?' Mike murmured, but

he was talking to himself.

So he began counting, mouthing the numbers at the pace the lassoers used when practising their act, while wondering what they planned to do.

He'd reached eight when he heard clattering above coming from two different directions. Then Dexter and Sheridan leapt from the roof. In a moment he realized what their plan was, but he didn't wait for it to happen. He kicked open the door, then threw himself through.

He hit the floor and rolled over a shoulder to come to rest on one knee facing the men inside. The five hired guns jerked round to face him letting him see that Nyle was behind them, questioning Brandon and Eve. The gunslingers shook off their momentary surprise, then swung their guns towards him.

Mike was already prepared. He fired at the central man, sending him spinning away, then turned his gun on the man beside him. He couldn't hope to get all the men, but at that moment Dexter and Sheridan came crashing through the windows on either side of him.

With a simultaneous motion they released the ropes on which they'd swung down from the roof. Then they dropped to their knees to cushion their fall. Torn between firing at these men or at Mike, the gunslingers hesitated.

The showfolk ensured that their hesitation was fatal.

Mike cut a swath of lead across the gunslingers in the middle, making them jerk backwards, their chests holed while Dexter and Sheridan picked out the men at the end. Repeated gunfire tore into them before they tumbled over.

Mike was pleased to see that he recognized at least two of the men as having been amongst those who had shot up the hired guns after the massacre at Harmony.

Gunsmoke swirled and eddied through the room, temporarily cutting off Mike's view of the back of the room. He winced when he heard a door slam. He got to his feet and ran past the fallen gunslingers to reach Brandon, who was jerking from side to side as he tried to decide whether to go after Nyle while unarmed.

'I'll deal with him,' Mike said.

'But he's got Eve,' Brandon said.

Mike patted Brandon's shoulder on the run, then stopped beside the door. He listened, hearing receding footfalls pattering down the corridor beyond.

He remembered that there was a door at the back and that from there Nyle would be able to reach the corral and escape. So he turned to Dexter and Sheridan.

'Go round the house and cut him off,' he said. 'I'll try to get him from inside.'

Neither man needed more details and they hurried off to the door. Brandon wavered for a moment then followed them. On the run he picked up a gun from one of the fallen men.

Mike pushed through the door, then flinched backwards when he saw unexpected movement. The motion saved him from a bullet that whined from the man on the other side of the door, the shooter being a hired gun he hadn't expected to be there.

Then the man was on him. He wrapped his arms around Mike's chest and slammed him back against the doorframe. All the air blasted from Mike's lungs, but he shook off the blow and pushed the man, sending them both into the corridor.

They tussled. Each man clamped his hands firmly on the other man's shoulders as they tried to drag each other down.

Neither man could get the upper hand, so they were turning on the spot. This at least let Mike see that Nyle was holding Eve at the other end of the corridor while keeping both them and the terrain beyond the door in view.

Mike presumed that this meant the showfolk had managed to cut him off, but it also meant a tense bargaining process would probably ensue. But first he had to subdue his assailant. The man was showing no sign of weakening as he bore down on him, then inexorably pushed him backwards.

The man slammed him against the wall, then again a second and a third time. On the last shove Mike jarred his elbow against the wall, sending numbing pain coursing down his left arm. The momentary weakness gave his assailant the advantage.

The man pushed him downwards. Then, in a surprising move, he released his grip, gripped his hands together and chopped them into the side of Mike's neck.

Mike hadn't felt pain in his jaw for some time, but this sudden blow gave him an unwelcome reminder of past agonies. He fell to the floor to lie there dazed and pole-axed. Groggily he looked up to see the man swinging his gun round to aim down at him.

Mike moved to turn his gun on him, but he was already too late. A gunshot blasted, echoing in the confined space.

Mike lay, feeling dumbfounded that he hadn't been hit.

He saw the man stagger to the side, then fall, to reveal a smoking hole in his back and Brandon standing behind him.

Mike didn't have time to be relieved that Brandon hadn't done as he'd requested. He swung round to face down the corridor, but it was to see Nyle with his gun held firmly up under Eve's chin.

'Keep that gun lowered,' Nyle ordered.

Mike got to his feet, but he did as ordered and kept his gun aimed at the floor. He avoided looking at Brandon in the main room, although Nyle would know he was there.

'What you hoping to do here, Nyle?' Mike asked.

'I'll do what I always do. I'll survive. You'll tell your friends outside to stand back. Then I'll walk through the door and to the corral. If you've got any sense, by the time I've rounded everybody up and returned, you'll be long gone.'

'Can't do that, Nyle.'

'You will if you don't want her to die like Jesse Cole did.'

Mike glanced down at his gun, then took a slow pace towards the pair at the other end of the corridor.

He snorted. 'You've not gone and got it into your head that I'm a lawman, have you?'

'We worked it out that you were Marshal Jesse Cole's deputy. That's why I sent Floyd after you.'

Mike rubbed his jaw, then barked out a harsh laugh.

'Except Floyd failed. His aim was poor, but mine's not, and that means you don't get to walk out of that door alive.' He took another pace. 'I'm going to blast you through it and before you hit the ground, you'll be filled with more holes than even Floyd was.'

Nyle sneered and dug the gun into Eve's skin, making her screech.

'Then it'll be alongside this dead woman.'

'Why should I care about that?' He

saw Eve wince, but he avoided meeting her eye.

'A lawman has to care,' Nyle murmured with the first hint of uncertainty in his tone.

'You're right. A lawman has to care about the people he swore an oath to protect, but the trouble is, you got it right the first time back in that trading post. I'm not a lawman. I'm just a hot-headed young gunslinger.'

'You can't be. You came with that US marshal.'

'I didn't know he was a lawman.' He gestured back down the corridor at the open door, signifying Brandon and the others. 'I mean, do you really think I'd risk the lives of these innocent showfolk to take you on when a lawman is supposed to protect people like them?'

'You're lying.'

'Maybe I am, but you'll find out the truth soon enough.' He snorted a laugh. 'So go on, kill her while I tear a hole in you.'

With deliberate slowness Mike raised

his gun, giving Nyle enough time to consider the hopelessness of his situation if he were to waste valuable seconds by killing her. Sure enough, with an aggrieved cry, he swung the gun away from Eve.

That was what Mike had waited for. He turned his slow movement into a quick snap of the wrist that flicked his gun up.

On the move he caught Nyle with a low shot to the guts that bent him double. As Eve dragged herself away from his grasp, Mike planted a second bullet in his chest that sent him crashing through the door as promised.

Then he paced down the corridor to stand in the doorway and look down at the body.

A relieved Eve stood behind him and placed a hand on his shoulder. The gesture said she understood why he'd acted as he had. But he kept his gaze on the man whom he'd been deputized to bring to justice.

He watched him twitch for the last time, then holstered his gun.

While the rest of the showfolk came scurrying into view and crowded round him, he turned his back on his duty and his old life and faced his new life.

'Thank you,' Eve breathed.

'It was a pleasure.' Mike took a deep breath. 'And I'm sorry I had to shoot your brother back at Prudence.'

'I know he gave you no choice, like this man.'

Mike nodded. 'You once asked me to take you away from the show. Is that what you still want?'

'Only if you don't want to stay.'

Mike considered, but before he could reply, Brandon poked his head through the door at the other end of the corridor.

'I reckon you should see this,' he said. 'I've found where Nyle Adams kept all his money.'

Brandon jerked back out of view. When he reappeared he was lugging a large open casket. From the contents

Mike could see that it contained a far larger haul of valuables than even Eve and Victor had accumulated.

'Now what,' Mike murmured, 'should we do with that?'

12

'What do you want?' the woman asked.

Brandon followed Mike and Eve in jumping down to face her. They considered the crude dug-out, then the other hovels lined up beside it. Other women along with children had emerged to see who had come to visit them. So far Mike had seen only a few men, and they were all old.

'You people took some finding,' he said, 'but we reckon we've come to the right place. Am I right in thinking you all used to live in a town called Harmony?'

'Yeah,' the woman murmured with a pronounced sneer.

'Then you would be Lily Hughes, George's wife?'

She narrowed her eyes as she considered Brandon, then turned to consider the wagons.

'I remember you. You performed for us just before . . . before it all ended.'

'We did,' Eve said, 'and we've come to tell you we visited Harmony again last week.'

'You shouldn't have bothered. There's nothing to see there no more.'

'But there is. Things have changed a lot.'

'Except for one thing,' Brandon said. 'The land still needs people and it sure is a better place to live than here.'

Lily shook her head. 'If you know what happened there, you'll know we can never return.'

'Never is a long time, but whatever you decide, we have something that might make starting afresh a mite easier.'

Brandon gestured and Dexter and Sheridan manoeuvred Nyle Adams's heavy casket from within a wagon and deposited it on the ground. They stood back to let Lily approach it, but her confusion as to their motives was controlling her movements. She backed away, then knelt beside her two children.

She put her arms around them. 'I don't know what you want of us or why you sought us out, but please just go and leave us in peace.'

'And we intend to do just that.'

Brandon backed away for a pace, leaving Mike to offer her a smile.

'I'll open it for you,' he said. 'Then we'll leave.'

He bent to the casket and flicked back the lid to reveal Nyle Adams's hoard, the accumulation of his activities over the last few years, much of which had presumably been gathered to the detriment of people like these.

Lily stood, catching a glimpse of the contents, as did the other former townsfolk of Harmony.

Tentatively they moved forward, the setbacks they'd suffered ensuring they all still looked doubtful.

Lily was the first to reach the casket. She drew out a handful of the valuables inside.

'You're saying that this is for us?' she murmured as the other townsfolk gathered around her.

'Nyle Adams wanted you to have it.'

The mention of his name made everyone back away, cringing. Lily threw her handful back into the casket.

'He can't buy us off.'

'He wasn't trying to.' Mike winked, then patted his holster. 'He didn't exactly give this up willingly.'

Understanding lit up her eyes. 'Are you saying he's dead?'

'All I'm saying is, when we left his ranch it was in an even worse state than Harmony was after his men had done their worst.'

Mike joined Brandon in climbing up on to the wagon from where he looked down at them.

Eve stayed to face Lily.

'Listen to what they're trying to tell you,' she said. 'Maybe if you were to head back to Harmony, you might enjoy what you find there.'

The townsfolk muttered to each

other, this time with greater enthusiasm and less scepticism. Then they moved in to explore the casket.

'Thank you,' Lily said. 'I don't know what else we can say.'

'Thanks is all we wanted,' Eve said, before she joined Brandon and Mike.

Lily came to the side of the wagon to look up at them. She offered Brandon and then Eve a smile, but when she faced Mike, she frowned.

'You weren't with the show when they performed before, but I recognize you.'

'Perhaps you do,' Mike said, finding that, despite the circumstances, this pleased him. She had recognized him from before his injury and that meant the scarring wasn't as bad as he had feared. 'I used to be a lawman. Now I'm Sharpshooter McClure, the finest shot in all the West, or so Brandon says.'

She continued to look at him, her narrowed eyes suggesting she was still searching her memory for an unwelcome recollection. The excited bleats of the townsfolk made her dismiss the matter with a shrug.

'Then I wish you good fortune wherever you may go, Sharpshooter McClure.'

Mike smiled then raised the reins. With a sharp tug he sent the wagon off.

After about 200 yards he allowed himself one last look back to see the eager townsfolk counting through the money they'd been given. Then he turned to the front.

'Where now?' he asked.

'I reckon,' Brandon said, looking at Mike from the corner of his eye to gauge his reaction, 'our next performance should be in Redemption City.'

Mike drew in a sharp intake of breath at the mention of the town where he'd been shot, encouraging Eve to lean over.

'If we're going to visit towns we've been to before,' she said, 'are you sure we should start there?'

'There will be trouble,' Brandon said, 'but as it'll be the same show as always, except without the stealing, it won't be anything we can't deal with.'

Mike agreed with a firm nod.

'All right,' he said. Then he considered some more and leaned towards Brandon. 'And if we're going to put on the same show, does that mean we'll still be performing the play?'

'We should continue to do it as a reminder of what happened in Harmony.'

'In which case can someone else play the gunslinger from now on?'

'That'll be acceptable.'

'And can I play the US marshal who's married to Eve?'

'Agreed,' Brandon and Eve said together.

'And I'd like some lines.'

'Maybe later,' Brandon said, smiling.

Mike returned the smile. Then, with a firm crack of the reins, he hurried the wagon on.

THE END